"I guess I have a lot to learn about you Amish," Leah said, taking a cup of punch from Ethan.

"Things are not always what they seem, Leah. Everyone here is free to try the things of the world. But we are still accountable to our families and our traditions."

"So I'm learning." She wondered what was going on inside Ethan, where he fit in in this strange no-man's-land of Amish tradition and English worldliness. She felt a kinship with him. They were both searching for a place where they belonged.

Lifted Up by Angels

Lurlene McDaniel

Lifted Up by Angels

BANTAM BOOKS
NEW YORK • TORONTO • LONDON • SYDNEY • AUCKLAND

RL 4.7, AGES 012 AND UP

LIFTED UP BY ANGELS

A Bantam Book / November 1997

The Starfire logo is a registered trademark of Bantam Books, a division of Bantam Doubleday Dell Publishing Group, Inc. Registered in U.S. Patent and Trademark Office and elsewhere.

Scripture quotations marked (NIV) are from the Holy Bible, New International Version. Copyright © 1973, 1978, 1984 by International Bible Society. Used by permission of Zondervan Bible Publishers.

ISBN 0-553-57112-5

Published simultaneously in the United States and Canada

Bantam Books are published by Bantam Books, a division of Bantam Doubleday Dell Publishing Group, Inc. Its trademark, consisting of the words "Bantam Books" and the portrayal of a rooster, is Registered in U.S. Patent and Trademark Office and in other countries. Marca Registrada. Bantam Books, 1540 Broadway, New York, New York 10036.

PRINTED IN THE UNITED STATES OF AMERICA

OPM 10 9 8 7 6 5 4 3 2

This book is dedicated to my friend
Mary Lou Carney—who took the notes!

"For he will command his angels concerning you to guard you in all your ways; they will lift you up in their hands so that you will not strike your foot against a stone."

(Psalm 91: 11-12, New International Version)

ONE

"Leah, this makes no sense to me. Why would you want to rent an apartment in a hole in the wall like Nappanee, Indiana, when you could be sailing to Fiji on a windjammer with Neil and me for the summer?"

Not bothering to answer her mother's question, Leah Lewis-Hall dragged her suitcase into the bedroom of the sparsely furnished apartment. She was seventeen, but if she lived to be a hundred, she still wouldn't be able to explain it to her mother. She'd tried before they'd driven from Neil's sprawling, wonderful farmhouse that morning, but her mother didn't get it. How come she couldn't understand that Leah did not want to tag along with her and

Neil, husband number five in her mother's life? An entire summer with them would never be her idea of fun. Not when she could be near the Longacre family, the kindest people she'd ever met: Rebekah, Charity, Ethan . . . Especially Ethan.

Leah's mother glanced disdainfully around the small room. "Good thing Neil had a friend in the real estate business up here, or I would never have let you come."

In spite of Neil's being many years older than her mother, Leah liked him. After six months of being married to her mother, Leah realized, Neil had a better understanding of her than her mother did. When Leah explained to Neil her plan and what it would mean to her, he had helped her get both a place to live and a job working at a bed-and-breakfast in Nappanee. Neil truly seemed to understand when Leah had flatly said to him, "I wanted to make my own summer vacation plans. It's been a rough year." The nine days Leah had had to spend in the hospital just before Christmas while her mother and Neil had been in Japan on their honeymoon were the toughest of her life. That was when she had been diagnosed with bone cancer.

"Dr. Thomas does want me in for another checkup at the end of June," Leah said now.

"They misdiagnosed you in the first place," her mother insisted. "You could come to the South Seas with us. You are fine now. That doctor just scared us to death."

Leah didn't know what to believe. Her early X rays and bone scans had clearly indicated that parts of her knee had been eaten away by cancer. Then, during her hospital confinement, Gabriella, a mysterious figure, had come into her life. Later X rays showed that the dark spots had shrunk even before any treatments. This had totally shocked her doctor.

"I went through six weeks of chemo for nothing then?" Leah asked her mother with a grimace.

"Insurance," her mother countered. "Besides, you did fine with chemo."

"Not much fun, though." Leah would never forget the bouts of nausea following each drug protocol. "Well, I'm here already. Neil understands, so why can't you?"

Her mother grabbed a grocery sack full of Leah's shoes and headed to the closet. "Can you cook well enough to even feed yourself?"

"I can cook. And I have Grandma's recipe

box." Her deceased grandmother was another sore subject between Leah and her mother, so Leah was glad when there was no comment. "I really will be fine, Mom. Stop worrying."

"I can't believe you'd rather clean toilets than sail to Fiji," her mother grumbled.

They'd already visited the small inn where she was to work. It was a two-story frame house with an old-fashioned parlor, family-style dining room and four quaint bedrooms and bathrooms upstairs. Leah would be responsible for fresh bed linen daily, cleaning chores, and serving breakfast and lunch to guests. Her workday would begin at seven A.M. and end at three every afternoon. She'd be off on the weekends.

"You'll be a *maid.*" Her mother chewed her bottom lip fretfully.

Leah rolled her eyes in exasperation.

Her mother tagged behind Leah as she went into the tiny kitchen. "Is your phone working? I sent in a deposit and told them to turn it on."

Leah picked up the receiver and held it out so that they could both hear the dial tone.

"I'll call and check on you before we drive to the airport tomorrow." Neil and her mother were to fly from Indianapolis to Los Angeles, then to Hawaii, where they would board the sailing vessel that would take them to the South Pacific island of Fiji.

"I'll be fine, Mother."

"Are you positive those Amish people will look after you? Don't you think I should meet them?"

"You read Charity's letter. She's glad I'm here for the summer. And no, you do not need to meet them." When Leah had first formed the plan to work in the area for the summer and had written Charity about it, Charity had written back to say it would be nice to see her again. Now that Leah was actually here, she hoped she'd not acted presumptuously.

"It just seems so . . . so . . . odd to go off and leave you, that's all." Her mother broke into Leah's thoughts. "And I can't believe you're so casual about living alone all summer. Even though the diagnosis was wrong, it still makes me anxious."

Leah sorted her mother's mismatched silverware into a drawer, knowing she was acting more self-assured than she felt. She reminded her mother that it was she who'd taught her self-reliance and independence in the first place.

"Mom, I'm going to have a good time this summer, and so are you and Neil. August will be here before we know it."

"You have the ship-to-shore phone number," her mother reminded Leah. "If you have any problems—"

"Don't worry," Leah interrupted.

"There's still time to change your mind, you know."

"I'm not changing my mind."

Her mother sighed and glanced at her watch. "Maybe we'd better buy some milk and things at the grocery store before I go."

"I can shop by myself. You'd better get on the road if you want to be home before dark." They'd driven up in separate cars, Leah's mother in the car Neil had given her for a wedding gift and Leah in the sporty red convertible he'd given to her after her last chemo session. "You deserve it," he had said, handing her the keys.

Her mother hugged Leah. "I'll miss you."

"Miss you too," Leah said. "Give a hug to Neil. He's really a nice guy, Mom. And don't get seasick."

Her mother made a face. "Don't even mention such a thing."

Leah walked her mother down to her car and waved goodbye when her mother drove away. Then she stood alone in front of the apartment building and hugged her arms to herself, blinking back tears. *No regrets,* she told herself. This is what she had wanted—to be on her own. And now she was.

Leah wasted no time going to the grocery store; instead she took out the roughly drawn map Charity had sent her and followed it to the Longacre farm. The Indiana countryside was flat, the road straight as an arrow as it passed fields of young corn plants. The late-afternoon sun felt warm on her head and shoulders, but although it was late May, the breeze still held an edge of coolness. In less than fifteen minutes, she turned off the main highway onto a gravel road marked as the entrance to the farm. Far back on the property, she saw a rambling two-story farmhouse. Of course, no telephone poles, no wires for electricity led up to the house. The Amish kept their own ways and did not want modern conveniences.

Leah stopped shy of the well-cared-for lawn.

The screen door banged open and Charity, gathering her skirt, darted off the porch. She wore a long, plain brown dress covered with a long white apron. The ties from her prayer cap flapped as she ran toward the car. "Leah, how pleased I am to see you!"

Leah scrambled from the car and embraced her friend, a lump of emotion clogging her throat. "You look wonderful!"

Charity stepped an arm's length away. "And you look beautiful. Too thin, I think."

"Left over from the chemo treatments. But I didn't lose much hair." Leah spun, and her dark hair, now shoulder length, fluffed in the breeze.

"You must tell me everything. But first, we must go out to the garden, where someone is waiting to see you."

Charity led Leah around to the back of the house, where two women and two girls were tending a large vegetable garden. Leah recognized Charity's mother, Tillie, at once. Upon seeing Leah, the child beside Tillie dropped her hoe and ran, arms outstretched to meet her.

"Rebekah!" Leah cried, catching the girl in her arms. "You've grown so big." She hadn't seen Rebekah since she'd left the hospital room they'd shared.

The six-year-old beamed a smile at her. One of her front teeth was missing, making her look even cuter than Leah remembered. "I thought you'd never get here. I've been waiting all day," Rebekah said.

"I'm here now," Leah answered with a smile.

Charity introduced her sister, twelve-year-old Elizabeth, and her grandmother, whom they called Oma. The baby, Nathan, now eight months old, lay asleep on a nearby blanket. "We shall all rest and take some lemonade," Tillie Longacre announced. "And you must join us for dinner tonight, Leah."

Holding Rebekah's hand, Leah followed the group to a wooden picnic table, where chunks of ice sparkled in a pitcher of lemonade. "Thank you. I'd like that," Leah said, feeling oddly out of place in her modern clothes. She was what the Amish called English. She was not one of the "plain people." She felt her differences keenly.

"I want you to come see my chickens," Rebekah said.

"I can't wait to see them. Actually, I don't think I've ever seen a live chicken up close and personal."

Everybody laughed.

Before her mother had married Neil and moved to his farm, Leah had lived in Dallas and attended a huge metropolitan high school. After the move, she'd experienced culture shock.

"Leah can visit your chickens later," Charity said. "Right now, I want her to walk with me to the barn."

"That's where Ethan is," Rebekah declared. "He's been looking for you all day too."

Leah saw a sidelong glance pass between Tillie and Oma. She wondered if they approved of her visiting Ethan. But she couldn't help the tingle of excitement that skittered up her spine at the thought of seeing him again. She recalled their bittersweet goodbye the previous December in the hospital lobby.

"Come with me," Charity said, setting down her glass of lemonade.

Leah abandonded her lemonade and followed Charity across a wide field toward a large gray barn. The closer they got, the more nervous Leah grew. What had Ethan been thinking? What if he didn't think she was pretty anymore? What if he'd decided his girlfriend, Martha Dewberry, was more to his liking because she was Amish? Ethan had written to Leah, but his wording had been stilted and

"I am fine. But it is not me we should be talking about. How have *you* been?"

"I made it through chemo and all. It really wasn't so bad."

"So the cancer in your bones is gone for good?"

Leah wasn't sure how to answer. More than anything, she wanted to believe it was gone. "I have to go for checkups every three months for two years. If there's no relapse, the doctors might pronounce me cured." She gave him the answer her doctor had given her mother when she had asked the same question.

"That is good. Have you seen Gabriella again?"

"No. And I don't think I will, either."

"If she was an angel from the Lord sent to heal you, it does not seem likely that she will appear to you again. There is nothing left for her to do for you."

"Everybody else thinks she was a nutcase who somehow slipped through hospital security. All I know is that before she came to see me that last time, I was facing having my leg amputated. After she touched me, my X rays started changing." Leah shrugged. "Maybe it was just a coincidence. I guess I'll never know for sure who she was."

"I am glad you will be working in Nappanee for the summer, because I will be able to see much of you," Ethan told her. "Charity told me where you will be working."

His assurance made Leah feel better. "I like the owners, Mr. and Mrs. Stoltz," she said. "There'll be another girl working with me, but I haven't met her yet. You and Charity will have to come visit me in town. I have a cute little apartment, not too far from the inn, and a car to get me there. No excuses for ever being late." Leah felt as if she was babbling, but she couldn't seem to stop.

"You will live by yourself?" He made it sound slightly scandalous.

"Sure I will. I can come out and pick you up if you want. Can you ride in my car with me?" She knew the Amish would use modern transportation when necessary. She wasn't sure if a visit to her apartment counted as necessary.

"I can ride with you."

"Of course, I'd like to ride in that buggy of yours sometime." Leah gave a nervous laugh. An Amish boy only asked a girl to ride in his buggy when he was interested in her romantically. It was Leah's way of asking if he still cared about her or if, since December, Martha had won him back.

He raised his hand as if to touch her cheek but drew back at the last second. "There is much I would like to do with you, Leah."

Her knees went weak. "I—I won't be in the way this summer, will I?"

"In the way?"

"You know. A bother, a pain."

"How could you be in my way? I want you near me."

The sound of running feet interrupted them. "There you are!" Rebekah exclaimed. "Ethan, can Leah come back to the garden now? She's staying for supper, so you can see her later."

"You are staying?"

"Your mother invited me." He looked solemn, making her ask, "Is it all right to have dinner with your family?"

"Oh yes. Please. It is good to think about seeing you at our dinner table tonight."

"Even though I'm English?"

He grinned. "I have eaten with you before. You are very civilized."

She returned his smile. "I promise not to throw my food."

Rebekah tugged on her hand. "Come. I'll show you the chickens on the way back."

Leah tossed Ethan one last glance and followed the little girl outside. The bright sunlight made her squint. She gazed around the beautiful stretch of farmland. Far back on the property, she saw another house. "Who lives over there?" she asked, pointing.

"My sister Sarah and her husband, Israel," Rebekah said.

"I remember." During their hospital stay, Rebekah had told Leah about her sister's Amish-style wedding: very different from most weddings.

"Yes, and guess what?" Rebekah lowered her voice, although there was no one around to overhear. "Sarah's going to have a baby." The little girl giggled. "Her stomach is fat. I saw my cat have kittens, so I know these things."

Leah suppressed a smile. "That'll make you an aunt. And your mother a grandmother. And your oma a great-grandmother."

Rebekah's eyes grew large. "I'll be an aunt?"

Leah stroked the child's head, which was covered by a black prayer cap, and remembered how she used to long for a sister when she was growing up. "Yes, you will."

After looking over the chickens in Rebekah's charge, Leah accompanied the girl to the house. They entered a spacious kitchen filled with the smells of baking bread, roasting meat, and simmering vegetables and gravies. A table, filled with mixing bowls and resembling a command center, stood in the center of the room. Cupboards reached to the ceiling along two walls, and a sink with a hand pump stood under a window. Leah saw Elizabeth toss wood into a large black cast-iron stove. The room was overly warm. Then she realized that the house had no electricity, so that meant, along with a woodstove for cooking, no air-conditioning or fans.

"Rebekah, set the table, please," Mrs. Longacre said.

"What should I do?" Leah asked when Rebekah had scurried away.

"Help me peel carrots," Charity answered.

Leah started scraping vegetables into the sink. "Ethan looks great," she told Charity quietly. "Thanks for letting us be alone together."

"He's been eager to see you."

Pleased, Leah said, "I wasn't sure. I mean, I know I'm not the ideal girl for him to bring home to Mom and Dad."

"Our family has had English here before."

"Really? Who?"

But Charity clamped her lips together, and bright spots of color appeared on her cheeks. "Forgive me. I should not have spoken of the past."

Leah knew they couldn't talk freely with Charity's mother and oma so close by, but she was puzzled. What did she mean? And why act so secretive about past dinner guests?

In an hour the meal was ready, and Mrs. Longacre stepped out on the porch and clanged a large bell. "Calling the men in from the fields," Charity explained.

When the men arrived, Charity introduced her family. "You remember Papa and Ethan. And this is my grandfather, Opa, and my brother Simeon."

Leah smiled at the Amish men without meeting Ethan's eyes. Mr. Longacre welcomed her, but his greeting seemed stiff and formal.

In the dining room a long table with straight-backed chairs took up most of the floor space. No pictures hung on the walls, no rug covered the hardwood floor. A pull-down shade was the only decoration on the window. Serving dishes, heaped with food, garnished the bare tabletop.

Mrs. Longacre hung an oil lamp from a low ceiling hook over the table and lit it with a long match.

Mr. Longacre took his seat at the head of the table, and the other men sat to his right in descending order of age. Mrs. Longacre took a chair on his left, and then the girls sat, with Leah between Charity and Elizabeth. Baby Nathan's high chair was wedged between the parents. Leah tried not to fidget.

"We shall thank God," Mr. Longacre said.

The blessing was brief and spoken in both German and English. The men passed the bowls among themselves first, then to the women. *No "ladies first" rules here,* Leah thought. The meal was quiet, the only sounds being those of bowls scraping against wood and utensils striking plates. When a bowl was emptied, Charity or Elizabeth, taking turns, went to the kitchen and refilled it. Leah thought the food was good, but she was too nervous to really enjoy the meal. She sensed tension in the room and wondered if her presence was the cause of it.

"Bud threw a shoe this afternoon," Opa said at one point.

"He'll have to be taken to the blacksmith," Mr. Longacre said.

"I can take him tomorrow," Ethan said.

"You have other tasks," his father replied.

"I will take the horse," Ethan said, surprising Leah. His tone almost sounded defiant—not at all Amish.

Ethan's father gave Ethan a hard look. The grandfather said, "Let him take the horse, Jacob. It is his choice."

Mr. Longacre gave an imperceptible nod, and although Leah knew something out of the ordinary had occurred, she didn't have a clue what it was. Her stomach continued to tighten, and by the time the meal was over and the table cleared, she wanted to jump out of her skin.

When the women began cleaning up and the men retired to the barn, Leah followed Charity out into the yard. Night had fallen, and without a porch light, Leah could hardly see two feet in front of her. Charity began to fill a large pot with water from the outside pump.

Leah caught her friend's arm. "Something's wrong, isn't it? Please tell me, Charity. What have I done to offend your family?"

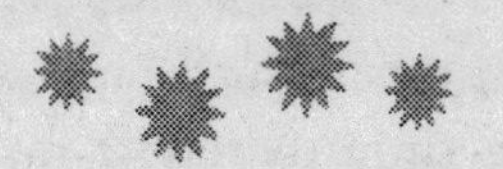

THREE

Charity set the pot down. "Whatever do you mean?"

"I could tell something was wrong tonight," Leah said in a rush. "Everyone hardly said a word at the dinner table."

"Oh, Leah, forgive me. I forget you are not accustomed to our ways."

"No, I'm not," Leah said, quietly. "And now I feel the differences more than ever. I'm English. Your family dislikes me. Maybe I'd better just go away."

"Do not say such a thing. My family *does* like you. You were so kind to Rebekah in the hospital. We will never forget that." Charity took Leah's hands in the dark. "Let me try to explain things to you. It is true we do not talk much at meals. For us, mealtime is not a time for idle chatter. It is a time to reflect on God's bounty and generosity to us."

"Your father and Ethan talked. And they didn't exactly sound happy, either. What's the big deal about taking a horse to get a shoe?"

Charity dropped Leah's hands. "Walk with me," she said.

Leah went with her to the edge of the yard, where the light from the kitchen windows dropped off. An old wagon wheel had been propped against a large rock and a flower bed had been planted around it. The sound of chirping crickets broke the stillness, and fireflies flickered in the darkness.

"Family is very important to us Amish," Charity said.

Family was important to Leah too. All her life she had wanted to belong to a family—a real family, not the kind her mother kept manufacturing. Her mother couldn't make any marriage work. She kept getting divorced, and she and Leah kept moving from place to place. Leah had never known her real father, and she had seen her beloved grandmother—also someone her mother didn't get along with—die of cancer. Leah still felt keenly the loss of her grandmother, her father, and the family life she'd never known. "I can see how close your family is," she said, "but I know there was something going on tonight between Ethan and your father. Is it me? Tell me the truth."

Charity didn't answer right away, and when she did speak, her words were halting, as if her thoughts were difficult to express. "Among us Amish, no man is baptized until he knows he wants to accept our ways and live according to all Amish traditions. After baptism, he becomes a church member. He marries and works. He obeys the church elders and lives simply."

Confused, Leah asked, "Why are you telling me this?"

"Because Ethan is not yet baptized."

"What does that mean?"

"It means that he still has freedom to choose what he wants to do with his life," Charity said quietly.

"What kind of freedom?" This news surprised Leah, for she had assumed that the Amish way of life was ordained from birth.

"When an Amish boy turns sixteen, he is free to experiment with worldly things. It is called *rumspringa*—'taking a fling.' All our fathers have done so, and they give their sons much leeway. Boys are exempt from chores and even church on Sundays. They are allowed to stay out all night on weekends with other Amish teens at parties and dances. Parents don't forbid this kind of thing because the Bible teaches that forbidden fruit becomes more appealing. Amish parents hope that if they look the other way, then their boy will eventually grow tired of the pleasures of the world and come back to simple ways. Most of them do."

Leah asked, "What about you girls? Do you 'experiment' too?"

"Yes."

"Have you?"

Charity was quiet, and Leah wondered if she'd pushed her friend too far. She'd already heard more than she'd bargained for. Finally Charity said, "I have played with my hairstyle. And put on makeup and worn English clothes. I—I have allowed a boy to kiss me."

Leah almost smiled. She'd been doing these things for years. But she could see that for Charity, such actions could be daring. "I'd like to hear about your boyfriend."

"You will not tease me?"

"Why would I tease you?"

"It is—" Charity stopped, then started again. "Sometimes teasing is done among us. I do like it. Ethan does not like it, but it is the way of our community. Others think it is funny to tease. That is why we keep our feelings inside. That is why we hide the things we do from others' eyes—even from our family. Especially when it comes to having a boyfriend or girlfriend. When a boy invites a girl to ride home in his buggy from Sunday-night singing, he is careful to conceal it from his friends, because they will tease him."

The implications of Ethan's asking Martha to ride in his buggy took on new meaning to Leah. If he would risk being teased by his friends and family, then he must truly care about Martha. Leah felt jealous of an Amish girl she'd never met or even laid eyes on. "And so, is Ethan starting to experiment? To test? Is that why your father sounded cross with him?"

"Ethan is testing, yes. But he does not tell me much. He keeps to himself, and none of us knows what he's doing. Or thinking." There was hurt in her voice.

"But Ethan is seventeen, and when we met in the hospital, he didn't seem to be experimenting." Leah had trouble accepting what

Charity was telling her because it went against everything she'd come to believe about the Amish. *All-night parties? No church attendance?*

"There were reasons why Ethan chose not to begin at sixteen, but I cannot speak of them."

That bothered Leah, but she couldn't force Charity to tell her. Instead she asked, "What other things do Amish boys do when they're taking their flings?"

"Some get fancy buggies. They buy radios and CD players. Some get driver's licenses and some even own cars. More liberal Amish parents allow the cars to be parked behind their barns."

"And these parents just pretend not to see it?" Leah was amazed. "What else?"

"They wear worldly clothing. Drink alcohol. Smoke," Charity answered, sounding uncomfortable. "Other worldly vices."

Like trying out worldly girls? The light of understanding turned on in Leah's head. She could be nothing more than an experiment to Ethan. She could be just a diversion in his fling-taking. She swallowed hard. "How about drugs?" she asked, embarrassed to let Charity know what she was thinking.

"Never. Well . . . I've never heard of anyone around here trying drugs. Boys are still expected to work on the farm or to take a respectable job in town or at a factory. They still live at home, and when at home they must be part of the family."

"How long do they get to experiment?" Leah kept her tone calm. Inside, she was still reeling.

"Until they decide to be baptized. Or leave the community."

Leah saw that Amish boys were no different than other boys she'd known. She felt disappointed.

As if sensing her disillusionment, Charity said, "Amish people are not perfect, Leah. We separate ourselves from the world, but what is easier? Giving up something you've never done, or choosing to live plainly *after* you have tried the English way of life? What good is a sacrifice if it isn't truly a sacrifice?"

The screen door opened and Charity's mother called for her to come inside.

Feeling guilty for keeping Charity talking instead of doing her chores, Leah said, "I guess I should be going."

"Since tomorrow is Saturday, we have many preparations to make for Sunday," Charity explained. "We don't work on the Sabbath, so everything must be done ahead of time. Tomorrow, I will make bread and rolls for Sunday dinner."

Leah realized that Charity wasn't inviting her to join them. "I start work Monday, and I have lots to do before then," she said, knowing it wasn't the truth. She had nothing to do.

Quickly Charity glanced over her shoulder. "Why don't you come to our Sunday-night barn dance? Amish kids will be there from all over. You can meet them."

"But I'm English."

"You will be welcomed because you are with us. We will ride together in Ethan's buggy. We will have a good time."

Leah wasn't sure she should tag along. But Charity's invitation sounded sincere. "Well . . . maybe . . ."

"Come to the house Sunday around six o'clock," Charity said hurriedly. "I must go inside now."

"Tell your Mom thanks for dinner," Leah called as Charity returned to the house. She stood in the yard for a few minutes, feeling alone, and wondering if she'd done the right thing by coming to Nappanee for the summer.

She couldn't stand the thought that her mother might have been right.

And now that Charity had explained about fling-taking, Leah was more confused than ever. Had all that she and Ethan shared in the hospital been part of some lifestyle experiment?

Leah went to her car. The brightness of her headlights made her squint. She turned toward the road, looking back only once. In an upstairs window, she saw a curtain move. In the window, backlit by a flickering lamp, Ethan stood peering out at her. Her heart ached. She gunned the engine and the tires spit gravel as she left the old road for the highway.

A phone call from her mother and Neil to say goodbye before they took off woke Leah on Saturday morning. After hanging up, she realized she'd never gone to the grocery store and didn't have a thing in the house to eat. She showered, dressed in jeans, grabbed her car keys and headed for the closest fast-food restaurant. After eating, she drove slowly around the town that was to be her home for the next three months.

Heads turned at the sight of her bright red car and made her feel self-conscious.

She saw Amish buggies in parking lots and in front of stores. They looked strange, dark and antiquated, amid all the modern cars and pickup trucks. The horses seemed unfazed by the noise of traffic. She pulled alongside a buggy at a traffic light, and the horse never gave her a glance. "Want to race?" she asked the uninterested animal.

Leah shopped for groceries, put the sacks in the backseat and headed to her apartment. Just as she pulled into an intersection, from out of nowhere, a boy wearing in-line skates zipped in front of her car. She hit the brakes hard. He threw his hands against her fender, careened backward, and landed hard on the asphalt.

Heart pounding, Leah cried out, turned off the engine and jumped from the car. "Are you all right?" She hurried to where the boy sat dazed on the ground. When she got to him, she gasped. Her car had just struck Simeon Longacre.

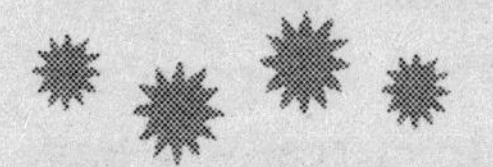

Four

"Simeon! Oh my gosh! Are you hurt?"

He reached for his broad-brimmed straw hat, which had been knocked off. "I am all right," he told her. But Leah saw that the palms of his hands were scraped and bleeding. His pant leg was torn.

Leah was shaking. "I'll take you to a doctor."

"No. I am fine. Please, do not worry about me." He struggled to his feet shakily, and she reached out to steady him.

"What are you doing out here anyway? And on skates?"

"I deliver small packages from the pharmacy on Saturdays to people who are shut-ins. Ethan brings me into town."

"Let me take you to get checked over. Please."

"No, I am fine, really. I have fallen before." He examined his skates. "I think they are undamaged." He started to push away from Leah. She caught his elbow.

"No you don't. In the car."

"I am fine. I can manage."

"No way. Where's Ethan?"

"At the blacksmith's."

"Tell me how to get there."

As she followed Simeon's directions, Leah fought to calm herself. What if she'd run over Simeon? *That* would certainly ice it with Ethan and his family! She glanced at Ethan's kid brother. "I didn't know Amish could own skates," she said above the drone of engine.

"They are allowed," Simeon said, poking curiously at the buttons on her dashboard. "Roller skates and ice skates have always been allowed. But these are the best because they are both."

"You know, maybe you should wear a helmet. Knee pads, elbow and wrist pads might not be a bad idea either," Leah said. "It's so much safer."

"Those things are showy. Not for plain people."

Leah was amazed by Simeon's logic, but she didn't argue with him.

Leah drove to the outskirts of town, turned onto a paved country road and followed it until Simeon pointed to an old barn set back from the road. She turned into a rutted driveway that led to the barn. An unhitched black buggy stood in front. From inside, she heard the sound of metal hitting metal. She saw Ethan holding the rope halter of a large draft horse while a man hammered an iron horseshoe on an anvil. An open furnace glowed red.

Ethan looked shocked as Leah and Simeon entered the barn. "What is wrong, Simeon?"

"We ran into each other," Leah said. "Literally."

The blacksmith nodded a greeting but didn't stop his work. Leah saw that he was Amish by his beard—full on his chin but with no mustache.

Briefly Simeon told Ethan what had happened. "Are you hurt?" Ethan asked his brother.

"No. And I have other errands to run for Mr. Fowler."

Ethan looked anxious, glancing back to the

blacksmith. "Um—I will be finished here shortly and can give you a ride back into town."

"I can give him a ride," Leah said. "Come if you want. I'll bring you back."

"I do not want to cause a burden for you."

"I offered, didn't I?"

Persuaded, Ethan helped his brother into the backseat and got into the front. Soon they were speeding down the road, radio blaring and wind whipping. Leah cut her eyes to Ethan, saw a look of pure exhilaration on his face and thought, *He likes cars.*

When they arrived at Simeon's place of employment, Ethan held the seat forward as his brother climbed out of the car. "I will return for you at four o'clock in the buggy."

Simeon thanked Leah, then skated around the side of the building.

"Simeon could have been badly hurt today when he fell," Leah said, checking traffic in her rearview mirror. "When I asked him about safety gear, he said you Amish consider it fancy. Is that true?"

"Some bishops do not allow their people to use in-line skates at all. We are fortunate that ours is more liberal."

"Do you skate?"

"Yes. And you?"

"Sure. Maybe we could skate together sometime."

"I would like that, Leah."

The way he said her name made goose bumps break out on her arms. What was it about him that affected her so? Why was she attracted to him when they had so little in common? On impulse, she asked, "Would you like to see where I live? My apartment isn't far from here. What am I saying? Nothing in this town is far from here."

He laughed. "The town is small, but still too big for many Amish. Too many tourists. They are always following us, taking pictures. It is annoying."

She knew that the Amish didn't like having their photographs taken. She wondered if Ethan still kept the one of her she'd given him in December. "I'm a tourist. Do I annoy you?"

"Oh, Leah, I am sorry. Not you. You are not annoying."

He sounded so stricken that she had to laugh. "I accept your apology."

"Yes," he said suddenly. "Yes, I would like to see where you live, very much."

She drove the couple of miles to her apartment, unlocked the door and flung it open. "Ta-da. Home."

He entered slowly, carrying the two bags of groceries she'd all but forgotten about. Many of her things were still in boxes, but the sofa was uncluttered. "Would you like something to drink?"

He nodded, setting the bags on the countertop that divided the living room from the tiny kitchen. She rummaged to find the soft drinks she'd bought. He asked, "May I look around?"

"Bathroom's that way, the bedroom beyond it. Excuse the mess." She put ice into paper cups while he explored. With a start, she remembered that her lingerie was lying all over the floor. And when Ethan returned to the kitchen area, the redness of his face told her he'd seen every filmy, lacy piece of it. She decided not to mention her unmentionables. "So, what do you think?"

"I think you are very fortunate to have such a place for your own."

"Even though it has electricity?"

"And running water too."

She smiled and handed him a cup. "I don't know how you Amish live without such stuff. I don't think I could."

"Charity tells me you will come to our barn dance tomorrow night." He changed the subject.

"Do you mind?"

"I would like it very much."

The intensity of his gaze again raised goose-flesh along her arms. "Charity says we'll ride over in your buggy."

"It is best not to take your car."

"Because I'm an outsider? That won't change whether or not I drive, you know."

"You will meet many tomorrow night who dress as you do, talk as you do, go to English schools and have many English ways. Do not concern yourself with your differences."

"But these different ones, are they still Amish?"

"Some are from less strict districts of Amish, but yes. The important thing is getting together, having a good time."

"Will your friend Martha be there?" She hated to ask, but she had to know.

"Yes," he said simply.

"I don't want people staring at me all night. They won't, will they?"

"If they do, it is only because you are so pretty."

"I'm just me," she said. "And to be serious, I'm not sure where I fit in in this world of yours."

"I do not know either. Yet you are here."

Leah stared into the cola-colored depths of her cup. Since her stay in the hospital, she had become fascinated by the Amish lifestyle. Not that she ever wanted to live without electricity and running water. But there was something appealing about the simplicity of it. "I'm looking into my future and can't see where I'm going. I graduate next year, and I don't know if I want to go on to college. My grades are so-so, but I could probably get in if I work hard next year. But that's the problem. I don't know what I want." She turned toward him on the sofa. "You're lucky in some ways. You know what you want. You know what's in store for you."

He studied her intently before saying, "You are wrong, Leah. I do not know what I want."

She blurted out, "But you're Amish. You told me you like being Amish."

"That does not mean that I don't want to try out English things."

Her heart began to hammer. "What things?"

"Things that make me hungry for what is not Amish."

Leah's chest felt tight. "What does your family think about your trying these things?"

"I have kept them a secret," he confessed reluctantly.

"But why? Charity told me that parents expect their kids to experiment."

His cheeks flushed. "I did not want to bring shame upon my father."

"When we met in December, you hadn't tried anything English. I remember the video games and the candy bars." She wanted to add *"and our kiss,"* but lacked the courage. "Why start now?"

"Things have changed since December. Please, I cannot talk about my reasons for deciding not to join in with the others until now."

Leah didn't press him. "So what things have you done?"

He reached out and stroked her face with his fingertips. His skin felt rough against her smooth, soft cheek. "I have met you."

She swallowed hard, feeling as nervous as she had when she was thirteen, the very first time she was about to be kissed. But she wasn't thirteen. And she had been kissed many times. She squared her chin, determined to tell him what she was feeling. "I don't want to be some kind of experiment, Ethan."

"I do not understand."

"I don't want to be some experience you're dying to have. You know—smoke behind the barn, drink beer, date an English girl."

Ethan looked shocked. "I am not this way, Leah. Yes, I have tried out some of the things you've said. All these things are frowned upon by my family. But I have never been with a girl I did not choose to be with. And since I met you last December, there is no other girl that I want as much as I want you."

The thudding of her heart made her hands tremble. He was telling her things she wanted to hear, but she wasn't about to jump in head-first. She didn't want to embarrass herself and say or do things that she might regret later. She and Ethan were as different as day and night. Their attraction for one another was real, but she couldn't hang her heart on an attraction. "This scares me, Ethan."

"I am scared too. But not enough to go away unless you tell me I must."

"I—I can't." She stared down at her hands.

"Then I would like to see you as much as I can while you are here this summer. Is this all right with you?"

It was more than all right, but the knowledge didn't make her feel carefree and lighthearted. The knowledge was heavy, weighted with an understanding: Ethan was special. If she gave him her heart, he would treasure it. And if he gave her *his* heart— She cut off her train of thought abruptly. "We have a whole summer," she said cautiously. "I'll be with you as much as you want. And when the summer's over, we'll decide where we go from here."

He raised her chin with his finger and peered into her eyes. His gaze pierced, but it held only honesty and trust. "Yes. This is what I want too." Then he brushed his lips softly over hers.

FIVE

When Leah returned from taking Ethan back to the blacksmith's, she busied herself with unpacking her remaining boxes and putting her rooms in order. Still, by Sunday evening, she was a bundle of nerves. She kept remembering their conversation. She kept seeing Ethan's face and hearing his voice. There had been times in her life when, once a guy showed an interest in her, she would drop him because the thrill had been only in the chase. It wasn't that way with Ethan. He was special to her in ways she didn't even understand.

When Leah arrived at the farm, she hugged Rebekah and then climbed into the small, enclosed black buggy with Charity and Ethan. She was careful not to sit too close to Ethan, careful to talk mostly to Charity while they were in the yard and in sight of Mrs. Longacre. Leah saw concern etched in the woman's face and figured Tillie Longacre didn't approve of the attachment of any of her children to Leah.

Ethan clicked with his tongue and slapped the reins against the horse's rounded rump, and the buggy headed for the gravel road. "The barn dance is at the Yoder farm, a few miles from here," he explained. "It will not take long to get there."

Sandwiched between Charity and Ethan, Leah felt like an oddity. They were dressed in Amish style, plainly. She'd chosen a long denim skirt and a solid white T-shirt and had worn only blusher and pale pink lipstick, but, compared to them, she thought she looked overdone. "I've never ridden in a buggy before," she said, making conversation.

"It is not fast like your car," Ethan said.

"Slow is good sometimes."

Charity asked, "Will you take me for a ride in your car as you have my brothers?"

"Whenever you want."

"I will have to come into town with Ethan for such a ride. My papa would not approve."

Leah didn't like being cast in the role of perpetually bad influence, but she hated to tell Charity no. Glancing at Ethan, she said, "I'd like to see those woods where your father cut the Christmas tree for our hospital floor."

"I will show the woods to you."

Darkness fell and Leah watched the stars come out. Eventually Ethan turned the buggy down a side road and Leah saw a farmhouse and a barn off in the distance, windows aglow with electric lights. "Is this an Amish farm? I see lights."

"The Yoders are not as strict as Papa," Charity said. "That is why so many like to gather here."

The barn was surrounded by buggies as well as automobiles. Music spilled from an open door. Ethan pulled back on the reins. The buggy lurched to a halt. He hopped out, tied the horse to a railing and came around to help his sister down. Then he reached up to help Leah. She stood, and the buggy swayed. "I'm not used to floors that keep moving after the vehicle stops," she said with a nervous laugh. The horse shifted, and Ethan's strong hands gripped her waist. He lifted her as effortlessly as if she'd been a doll. She stood on the ground facing him, his hands still encircling her waist, and for a moment she could scarcely catch her breath. He smelled fresh and clean, like soap. He'd left his hat on the seat, and his homespun shirt was open at the neck, making him look less Amish. *For my sake?* she wondered.

Once inside, Leah tried to ignore all the eyes that stared, the heads that turned. The gathering was large, full of kids in their early teens, dressed in a mix of plain Amish and modern clothing: jeans, denim shirts, khaki slacks and stylish T-shirts. She felt as if she'd stumbled into a stage production where everyone was in costume. The animated conversation from the different groups slowed as people checked her out. Ethan gripped her hand, and he and Charity led her over to a cluster of girls dressed Amish-style.

"This is my friend Leah," Charity explained. "You know, the one I told you about from the hospital."

The girls were polite, but curiosity burned in their eyes. In the background, conversation grew louder and someone put on a CD. Funky music blared from speakers set up in the corner of the barn.

"Come," Ethan said. "We'll get some cookies."

Leah was certain she'd never choke one down, but she went with him to a long table filled with refreshments. From the corner of her eye, she saw a group of boys at the end of the table. Several were holding beer cans. "Are they drinking beer?" she asked.

"Yes. Some of the boys sneak it in sometimes," he said, giving a disapproving look. "But it should not be here." He looked at her. "If you'd like one, I can get it for you. I know they have more outside."

"No way. I hate the taste of the stuff." Leah was surprised to see the boys drinking. "I guess I have a lot to learn about you Amish," Leah said, taking a cup of punch from him.

"Things are not always what they seem, Leah. Everyone here is free to try the things of the world. But we are still accountable to our families and our traditions."

"So I'm learning." She wondered what was going on inside Ethan, where he fit in in this strange no-man's-land of Amish tradition and

English worldliness. She felt a kinship with him. They were both searching for a place where they belonged.

Three of the boys dressed English-style drifted over to them. They stopped in a semicircle in front of Leah and Ethan. The biggest guy, standing over six feet with hands the size of footballs, spoke to Ethan in German. Ethan answered in German in a tone that sounded sharp. Then Ethan said, "In English, Jonah. Say what you want to say in English."

Jonah acknowledged Leah with his eyes. "It is not common for English to attend our parties," he said. "Especially English that nobody knows."

She squared her chin. "I'm Leah Lewis-Hall, and I'm working and living in Nappanee this summer. I do know some people here. Not you, though. Glad to meet you." She smiled, although her insides quivered like jelly.

"And I am Jonah Dewberry. My sister Martha is over there." He pointed to a row of chairs where several girls sat looking at them. Martha wore jeans, boots, and a blue T-shirt. Her long dark hair hung loose down her back. With dismay, Leah saw that she was quite pretty.

Martha gave a little wave, and Ethan nodded at her, then turned back to Jonah. "Now that we have all met, perhaps you will move out of our way," Ethan said.

Jonah moved aside, and Ethan stepped around him, taking Leah with him. "Ethan," Jonah said, "tell me, do English girls *schnitzel* as well as Amish girls?"

Ethan's face turned bright red. "You must find this out on your own, Jonah," he replied evenly. "If you can find an English girl who will *schnitzel* you."

Jonah's face reddened. He leaned closer. "I have another question. Now that you are dating English, will you become one of us?"

"I am one of you."

"You still dress Amish. You still hold yourself apart. Separate. You are proud."

Leah knew that to call an Amish person proud was an insult, and she could see by the way Ethan stiffened that the remark had hit home. She held her breath.

Ethan turned and looked Jonah directly in the eye. "What I do is my business. Who I decide to be with is my choice. I am leaving with Leah now. Will you take Charity home for me?"

Jonah nodded. "If she will come with me."

"If you ask her, she will go."

Once outside, Leah stopped short. She was glad to be out of the barn, but she felt confused. "Wait a minute, Ethan. I don't get it. At first I thought you and Jonah would come to blows. I mean, most of the guys I know would have been swinging fists at each other by now. It's clear to me that Jonah didn't like you bringing me here. He thinks you should be with his sister."

"I do not care what he thinks." Ethan helped Leah into the buggy and untied his horse from the railing. "Jonah is Amish. I am Amish. Amish do not fight, no matter what. Not even in wars for the country. It is our way."

Leah settled onto the hard buggy seat. "But you were angry with each other."

"That is true."

"So why did you ask him to take Charity home? That doesn't seem like a nice thing to do to her."

"Jonah cares for my sister." He clicked his tongue and the horse went forward. "He would jump at the chance to be with her."

"But what does Charity want? Maybe she didn't want to go home with that—that Neanderthal!"

Ethan chuckled. "Oh, she likes Jonah Dewberry very much. He has taken her home in his buggy many times, but lately he runs with older, wilder boys. Boys who may not return to Amish ways."

Leah sighed in exasperation. The whole thing sounded like a soap opera to her. "Is Jonah her boyfriend? I mean, does *she* like this guy? He seemed very unfriendly."

Ethan slipped his arm around Leah's waist and pulled her closer to him on the buggy seat. "He is jealous because I came with the prettiest girl."

Leah accepted his compliment silently, knowing it wasn't the truth. She'd been around enough to know that the Amish kids weren't going to welcome her into their midst regardless of who had invited her to come along. It might turn out to be a long summer!

Lost in thought, Leah listened to the clopping of the horse's hooves on the roadway and watched the late-rising moon peek from behind a cloud bank. She recognized the Longacre property as the buggy turned onto it and felt a twinge of disappointment. Although the dance had been a flop, she'd hoped that their evening together might have lasted longer.

Ethan didn't drive the buggy to the place where her car was parked. Instead, he took them across a bumpy field toward a wooded area. At the edge of the tree line, he halted the buggy, hopped out and helped Leah down. "Come," he said. "I will show you a place like no other."

She followed him through the woods. A soft summer breeze stirred through scented pine needles, making a whispery, papery sound. They came into a clearing where a giant rock rested on a cushion of leaves and needles. He lifted her up and settled her on top of the boulder.

"This is my favorite place," he said. "Here, I feel peace. Whenever I am confused or angry, this is where I come."

She turned her face heavenward. A thousand stars twinkled above her. Moonlight bleached the ground snowy white. "It's really beautiful, Ethan. This is where the Christmas tree came from, isn't it?"

"Yes." He stood gazing down at her, his face lit on one side by the silvery moon.

Leah said, "It's more like a church than some churches I've been in. I've been going to a church back home, you know." She wasn't sure why she was telling Ethan this, except that she knew his faith was important to him. "I figure I owe God something, I mean, since my bout with cancer and all." She reached for Ethan's hand and rested it on the knee where her cancer had been discovered. The warmth from his palm spread through the material of her skirt. "I'm glad you were there for me. I'm not sure how I would have made it if it hadn't been for you and Charity."

"Knowing you has been special to me, Leah." He touched her hair.

Her heart skipped a beat. "I'm sorry your friends don't approve of me."

"I do not care what my friends think."

"What did Jonah mean when he said *'schnitzel'*? Is it a bad word?"

He chuckled. "It's a made-up word that some Amish use for 'kissing.' An older Amish girl usually kisses—*schnitzels*—a boy when he turns sixteen."

She felt the stirring of jealousy. Had the kiss she and Ethan shared in the hospital truly been his first? "So tell me, do I measure up? Do I *schnitzel* as well as an Amish girl?"

He cupped her face in his rough, work-worn

hands. "I do not know. You are the only girl I have ever kissed."

Her body began to tingle. "It's hard to believe you weren't kissed before."

"It is the truth." He offered no other explanation.

Leah burned with curiosity to know why not.

"But," he said, "I want very much to kiss you now."

All other thoughts fled her mind. She slid off the rock to stand facing him. "I would like for you to kiss me." She raised her arms to encircle his neck.

He pulled her body closer, pressing his hands against the small of her back. He lowered his mouth to hers, touching her lips with a velvet softness that left her dizzy. And longing for more.

Six

"Hi. I'm Kathy Kelly. You must be Leah." A cute girl with a tangle of brown curly hair grinned at Leah.

Leah returned the smile. "I guess we'll be working together."

The two of them stood in the hallway of the Sunshine Inn Bed and Breakfast, dressed in the shapeless uniforms that Mrs. Stoltz insisted her helpers wear. Kathy said, "This is my second summer working at the inn. I'll only be here through July Fourth weekend, though. Then I'm off to cheerleading camp. How about you? You ever do this kind of work before?"

"No. I worked in a fast-food place when I lived in Dallas."

"Dallas—wow, lucky you. I've been stuck here in Dullsville since my parents moved here when I was in seventh grade. I'm saving for college. How about you?"

"Just living here for the summer."

"You mean you *chose* to spend the summer here?"

"It's a long story." Leah certainly didn't want to go into her life history at the moment.

"You're not Amish, are you?"

Leah shook her head.

"Me either." Kathy rolled her eyes.

"What's wrong with being Amish?"

"Nothing . . . if you like being ignored. I went to school with some of them and they sure keep in their own little circles. Tight as gum stuck to your shoe."

"Do you know the Longacres? I'm kind of a friend of theirs." Leah wanted Kathy to know that she didn't want to hear her trash the Amish.

"Oh, don't get me wrong," Kathy said. "I like a lot of the Amish kids, but no matter what you do, you'll always be an outsider to them. They don't really have much use for us English."

Kathy's words felt like a splash of cold water to Leah. Was she fooling herself about Ethan?

The night before, he had kissed her in the moonlight until her blood fairly sizzled and her knees went weak. And he'd told her he would see her every chance he got. Now Kathy's remarks were making her wonder.

Kathy tipped her head and puckered her mouth in thought. "Longacre . . . Let me think."

"Ethan and Charity," Leah supplied.

"I sort of remember Ethan. He was in eighth grade when I started in seventh. He was really cute. But the Amish kids hardly ever stay in school beyond eighth grade, so once they're out of middle school, we don't see much of them. You interested in Ethan?"

"Sort of," Leah said.

"Well, good luck, if you have a thing for him. Really strict Amish parents never let their kids mingle with the likes of us."

Leah felt an enormous letdown. She didn't have time to dwell on it, however, because Mrs. Stoltz dashed out of the kitchen and started issuing orders about the day's work. Soon Leah was up to her elbows in soapy water. She and Kathy changed bed linens, scrubbed bathrooms and washed windows the entire morning. Mrs. Stoltz clucked her tongue over every streak they left behind and every piece of brass that didn't sparkle. She told them that the next day they would have to work faster. When Leah went to her car, she felt ready to collapse from exhaustion.

"The first day's always the hardest," Kathy told her as they stood in the small parking lot adjoining the inn. "And Mrs. Stoltz is pretty nice once she sees that you're trying to do a good job and not goofing off."

Leah rubbed the back of her neck. "Who had time to goof off?"

Kathy laughed. "See you tomorrow. Oh. Here's my phone number if you ever want to do anything on weekends."

Leah took the piece of paper Kathy handed her and got into her car. *Weekends.* She remembered Ethan's promise to spend as much time as he could with her, but after what Kathy had said, Leah wondered if it was going to be possible. Absently she rubbed her knee. It felt sore. Fear jolted her. The soreness was in the same knee where bone cancer had been discovered. *It's nothing,* she told herself. *I just overworked it today.* She threw the car into gear and screeched out of the parking lot.

Because Charity and Ethan had no phone, Leah couldn't call. She had no way of knowing if they missed her or even thought about her. On Friday, she drove to the farm. She had hardly shut off the engine when Rebekah came racing to the car, her long skirt flapping behind her. "Leah! Come quick! I have something to show you."

Leah jogged behind the little girl all the way to the henhouse. Inside the low wooden building, the warm air smelled like chickens and chicken feed. "Wow, this place needs some air freshener," Leah joked. "What's so important?"

Rebekah took her over to a small, wooden, bowl-shaped trough. "Look." The trough was an incubator, and in it eggs were in various stages of hatching. Rebekah scooped up a fuzzy baby chick and handed it to Leah. "Are they not wonderful?"

"He's cute, all right." Leah cradled the soft yellow creature against her cheek. The downy feathers tickled. Below, the others peeped noisily. "So now you have even more chickens to look after."

"Would you like to have one for your very own?" Rebekah asked.

"How can I keep it at my apartment?"

Rebekah thought for a moment. "I will keep it here for you. I will feed it and take care of it. But it will always be yours, Leah. And you can come visit it whenever you like."

Leah's heart melted at the girl's sweet gesture. "Thank you, Rebekah. This is the nicest present anyone has ever given me."

"I told Charity you would like my present. She said she didn't think a grown-up English girl would like a chicken, but I knew you would because you're my friend. You helped me in the hospital, even when no one made you help me."

"Do you remember the hospital?"

"Oh, yes. I remember the shots and the Christmas party and the funny bed that moved up and down." Rebekah giggled. "I liked to push the buttons and make it move."

"Do you remember Gabriella? The nurse who sometimes came to visit us?"

"She was pretty," Rebekah said. "She held my hand when I was scared and when you were asleep."

Leah was glad that someone else had seen the

elusive Gabriella. There were times when she wondered if she'd imagined her. "Gabriella helped me too."

"I can't wait to see her again," Rebekah said confidently.

"How do you know you will?"

"She told me so the night before I went home."

Leah figured that Charity and Ethan had not shared with Rebekah Leah's ideas about Gabriella's being an angel. If they had, Rebekah would certainly have mentioned it to Leah by now. "Well, tell her hi from me if you do see her," Leah said. "Where's Charity?"

Rebekah slipped her hand into Leah's. "Everybody's in the kitchen making jelly. We can help."

Leah hesitated. She wasn't sure she'd be wanted, but Rebekah fairly dragged her into the farmhouse kitchen. She found the women in the family hovering over pots boiling on the woodstove. Charity was washing jars in the sink and lining the clean ones up on the countertops and tables. "Leah!" Charity said. "How nice you are here."

Leah shifted from foot to foot self-consciously. Tillie and Oma smiled at her, but she thought the smiles looked stiff. "I'll just stay a minute. You look busy."

"We make jelly a couple of times during the summer. And we put up vegetables from our garden so we'll have plenty to eat during the winter," Charity explained. "Soon Rebekah, Simeon and a few of their friends will set up a roadside stand for the tourists to buy what we don't use."

"I guess I'm used to just going to the grocery store and buying what I want," Leah said. "My mother didn't cook very much when I was growing up because she worked."

Leah saw Charity's mother and Oma exchange glances. She recalled how Charity had spoken about Amish women and their devotion to home and family. "Of course, Mom had to work," Leah added defensively. "Sometimes I'd cook supper. I have my grandmother's favorite recipes. Maybe you could come over sometime and we could bake bread or something."

Charity flashed Leah a big smile. "That would be fun for me."

Charity's mother asked, "Would you like to help us make jelly now, Leah?"

"Sure," Leah said, surprised by the offer. She really wasn't looking forward to going back to her tiny apartment and spending the evening alone. "What should I do?"

Tillie led her over to a large basket of green apples. "You can peel these. And when we're finished, you can take some jars of jelly home with you."

"Thanks," Leah told her, and set to work, grateful to be busy. Grateful to be a part of the busy household, if only for a few hours.

Leah was putting gasoline in her car later that evening when she encountered Jonah Dewberry filling up a battered green car at the pump in front of her.

"Hello, Leah," he said cordially. "Do you remember me?"

"It's Jonah, isn't it?"

He nodded. "How are you liking your stay?"

"I'm liking it fine, so far."

"I saw your car out at the Longacre farm this afternoon."

"I was visiting." She didn't fully trust Jonah and didn't want to get overly chatty with him.

"Ethan speaks well of you."

"Oh? What does he say?"

"That you are . . . different. Special." But before Leah could feel pleased, Jonah added, "For English."

She stiffened. "I can't help who I am, Jonah."

He pulled the gas nozzle from his car, put it away and screwed on his gas cap. "The elders have a saying that we are taught from the time we are small children. It is, 'If you only date an Amish girl, you can only fall in love with an Amish girl.' "

His rebuke stung. "Do you mean, 'Play safe'? Do you always play safe? Don't you do things you're not supposed to do? I thought that was the whole point of taking a fling."

"My family would not approve of all that I do. But I have never brought home an English girl. It is a kind of fire that I know better than to play with. There are many Amish girls to pick from. I know one day I will want to be baptized, and marry, and have a family. Be careful, English, that you do not take my friend where it will be impossible for him to get back home."

Stunned into silence, Leah watched Jonah climb into his car and drive away.

SEVEN

Back home Leah usually slept in on Saturday mornings. But that Saturday, the ringing of her doorbell startled her awake. She grabbed her robe and stumbled to the door, peered through the peephole and saw Ethan standing on her doormat. She unlocked the door and pulled it open. "Well, hello," she said, not hiding her surprise. "I didn't expect you."

He took a step backward. "I am sorry. I have awakened you."

"It's okay. Really. Come in."

"I have come to call on you." He held his straw hat in his hand.

Leah glanced out the door, half expecting to

see his buggy down in the parking lot. "How did you get here?"

"I caught a ride with a farmer headed into town."

She rubbed sleep from her eyes. "Give me a few minutes." She hurried off to make herself more presentable, returning quickly dressed in jeans and a T-shirt, her teeth and hair brushed. "You want a soda? I start every day with one." She felt unnerved. She'd not seen much of Ethan since their night in the woods in the moonlight. Suddenly, here he was, acting as if no time had passed.

He followed her into the shoe-box-sized kitchen. "I came too early. I waited as long as I could, but I wanted very much to see you. I did not mean to wake you."

She glanced at the clock. It was ten A.M. "What time do you get up?"

"Five-thirty."

She groaned. "That's indecent. I can hardly get myself to work at seven every morning."

"I would like to call on you tomorrow too," he said.

She took a gulp of soda. "But tomorrow's Sunday. Don't you have church?"

"I have decided not to go."

The news sobered her. She knew what it meant. "Your family might not like this decision."

"Papa is not pleased. But he knows it's my right."

"Ethan . . . Are you sure about this?" Her run-in with Jonah came back to her. She felt guilty. Would Ethan have made this choice at this time if it hadn't have been for her?

"I know what I want, Leah."

Momentarily overwhelmed by emotion, she handed him a soda and walked back to the sofa. She noticed a large bag bearing the name of a department store propped against a cushion. "Yours?" she asked.

"I bought these things last week. May I use one of your rooms?"

"Sure. Use the bathroom."

She waited on the sofa, thoughtfully sipping her soda. She looked up and stared when he emerged. His Amish clothes had been exchanged for jeans and a blue chambray shirt, his wide suspenders for a belt with a shiny silver buckle. "You look great," she told him.

He seemed pleased. "Not Amish?" He sat on

the sofa with her, holding his homespun clothing rolled up in a ball on his lap.

"Less Amish."

"How can I look less so?"

She frowned. "Ethan—"

"It is what I want." His eyes, made even bluer by the hue of the shirt, were serious.

She cleared her throat. "You probably need a stylist to cut your hair."

"Ma and Oma have always cut my hair. What should it look like?"

"We can look through some magazines at guys' haircuts. There's got to be a stylist in town who can cut—"

"I cannot!" Ethan interrupted. "Not in Nappanee. It would shame me."

She thought for a moment. "Look, I have to go in for a checkup in Indianapolis at the end of the month. Maybe you could come along and get your hair cut there."

His expression turned to one of concern. "You should not have to go for this checkup alone."

"It's no big deal," Leah said, but deep down she knew it wasn't the truth. She was scared about the checkup. Often her knee throbbed at the end of the workday. She didn't want bad news from her doctor. And she certainly didn't want to hear it by herself.

Ethan scooted closer. "My haircut is not important. Would you like me to go with you to your appointment?"

"I'll have to go during the week because of testing. What about your farmwork?"

"I wish to be with you, Leah."

"I'm supposed to get a letter telling me when to report, so I'll let you know. Thanks so much, Ethan. It's nice of you to offer." She felt greatly relieved at not having to go by herself. "I plan to see Molly—you remember her, don't you? The nurse who was so nice, whose sister's diary Gabriella helped us find?"

"I remember her."

Leah took the bundle of clothes from his lap, running her palms over the rough weave of the white shirt and black trousers. The pants had no cuffs and only buttons, no zipper because zippers were considered prideful. She wondered if Ethan could put off his Amish upbringing as easily as he had the clothing. She picked up the bag, saw several other shirts and pairs of pants and dumped the old clothes inside. "So," she said, "what would you like to do today?"

"Isn't that a VCR machine?" He pointed to the piece of equipment sitting on the shelf under her TV set.

"Sure is. Neil insisted I have one in case I had nothing to do when I wasn't working."

"Can we rent some movies? I have been with my friends and seen movies before, but now I want to see many more."

"We can go as soon as the video store opens. But first, how about breakfast? I haven't eaten, and if you've been up since five-thirty, you must be hungry."

They went to the closest fast-food restaurant, where Leah ordered a biscuit and a soda and Ethan ordered pancakes, biscuits, eggs, bacon, two cartons of milk and a container of orange juice.

"You're going to eat all that?" she asked when they were settled at a table.

"Isn't it good to eat?"

"Of course, but I'd weigh as much as your horse if I ate like that."

He laughed. "You are prettier than any horse, Leah."

She giggled. "Thanks. I think."

Leah drove with Ethan to the video store after breakfast. Together they pored over the titles. If he picked up one she thought might embarrass them both, she shook her head. Once they returned to her apartment, she made popcorn and popped a video into the machine. They sat on the floor and spent the afternoon nibbling on snacks and watching movies. Leah couldn't decide what was more interesting—watching the movies or watching Ethan watching the movies. He mostly laughed at sight gags and pratfalls, rarely at verbal humor. Sometimes he even asked her what an actor meant in a scene with dialogue. His naïveté and unworldliness amazed her, and even though he'd told her once that he'd tried English things, she began to wonder just how much he'd actually done. Still, it felt good to be with him.

When they had watched three movies in a row, afternoon had turned into evening. Ethan said, "I am hungry. Where shall we go to eat supper?"

"You've been eating all afternoon." Leah felt slightly ill from her pig-out on junk food. "How can you be hungry?"

He shrugged. "It's a mystery, but I am." A grin split his face. "Let us try another place with fast food."

She groaned, but minutes later they were driving down the road in the convertible. "You just like riding in my car," she said above the *whoosh* of the wind.

"I like everything I do with you."

"Tell me, what are your friends doing tonight?"

"The Amish like to go to The Rink. But so do the English. It's a roller rink and game room. Turn right at the next light and I will show you."

She drove into a parking lot filled with cars and Amish buggies. Several of the buggies looked less than plain. They bore tassels and reflective tape cut in fancy designs. The harnesses were studded with ornamentations. Even the horses looked fancy. "Excuse me," Leah said, "but are those Amish buggies, or did space aliens drop into this place?"

"Aliens?" Ethan's brow puckered. "Oh, Leah, you are making a joke. No, the buggies belong to Amish. Some make their buggies fancy. Their parents do not like it, but they do not forbid it. It is our way."

Our way was becoming increasingly peculiar to Leah. What she had once thought taboo for the Amish was considered all right if done at certain times in their lives. Or, at least, parents and elders looked the other way while the kids did it.

Leah heard music blaring from the skating rink. Inside, the old-fashioned wooden floor was crowded with skaters. In an adjoining room, game tables were set in rows and kids were shooting pool. A selection of video games lined one wall. People looked up as Ethan and Leah came in. Leah was given the once-over. A couple of boys had the nerve to wink at her. But if Ethan was uncomfortable, he didn't show it. He walked her over to a table where several couples were shooting pool. "Leah, do you remember my friends from the dance?"

She said she did even though she didn't—except for Jonah and his sister Martha. She remembered *them* very well.

"So, Ethan, you have decided to join us," Jonah said. He eyed Ethan up and down while rubbing chalk onto the tip of his cue.

"I have decided to be with my friends this summer," Ethan said.

"All of your friends?" Jonah asked.

"The ones who matter to me," Ethan said.

Leah wondered if Jonah and Ethan could ever be friends.

Martha stepped forward. "We have missed you, Ethan."

Leah felt her cheeks redden. Martha ignored her as if she weren't even standing there.

"Good," Ethan said, slipping his hand into Leah's. "Then you will not mind if my friend Leah joins us at our parties."

Without blinking, Martha said, "Leah is welcome."

But Leah didn't feel welcome. She felt like an intruder.

"Would you like to shoot a game of pool?" Jonah asked.

"No," Ethan said. "We have been watching videos all afternoon on Leah's machine. We came here to eat."

Jonah studied Leah. "Perhaps we can all come over and watch videos sometime."

"Maybe," she said evasively.

"Ethan, will Charity ever come to watch videos with you?" Jonah asked.

"If she wishes."

Jonah nodded. "I will ask her."

Leah and Ethan walked over to a booth and

ordered a pizza. While they were waiting, Leah said, "I can't figure out what Charity sees in him."

"He is Amish," Ethan said with a shrug.

"There are plenty of Amish guys around. Why him?"

"This you will have to ask my sister. But everybody knows that once Jonah has had his fling, he will return to Amish ways."

She had heard this from Jonah himself. "Do guys ever not return to Amish ways?"

"Yes," he said quietly. Color crept up his neck, and Leah knew there was something he wasn't telling her. But what? She wanted to ask, but she didn't. There was something neither Ethan nor Charity seemed to want to tell her. It maddened her, but she swore she wouldn't pry. If Ethan trusted her, he would tell her. She would wait. If it took all summer, she would wait for him to open his heart totally and tell her the secrets of his soul.

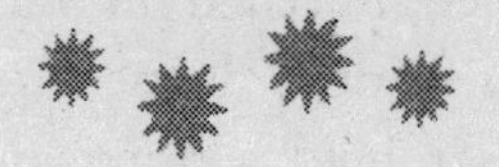

EIGHT

Leah's weekdays fell into a routine. She worked hard alongside Kathy, she returned to her apartment and crashed. She lived for the weekends. Leah had lived in Nappanee over a month when Ethan brought Charity to Leah's apartment. He promptly left so that the girls could visit with one another. "Leah, this is lovely!" Charity exclaimed as she walked from room to room. "So fancy."

"I'm glad you like it."

Leah had seen Charity's room, one she shared with Rebekah. It looked plain, almost austere, with no rugs or curtains. It contained only a double bed and a dresser. The bed was covered with a handmade quilt, a gift from Oma, Charity had explained. Perched on the bed was Rose, Rebekah's Amish doll, dressed in Amish clothing. The dresser held a hurricane lamp and a pitcher and basin used for washing up. There were no pictures or mirrors on the walls. The closet held six solid-colored cotton dresses for each of them. Wall hooks held long aprons and extra caps. Charity had explained that her winter dresses were packed away in a trunk, along with her winter cape. A single cross-stitch sampler of Scripture verse lay on a wooden rocker by the window.

Seeing Charity next to Leah's TV set, stereo, modern appliances and fixtures caused the gap between their lifestyles to stand out more than ever for Leah. By now, Leah was so used to Ethan's dressing English-style—for he never came to see her unless he was wearing his modern clothes—that Charity looked oddly archaic. "Sit. Have a soda," Leah said.

Charity perched on the couch and picked up the small pillow she had embroidered and given to Leah the Christmas before. "You have kept this?"

"It's one of my favorite presents." Leah took the pillow and ran her fingers over the finely stitched letters of her name. "Of course, it's nothing compared to Rebekah's chicken."

Charity laughed. "Leah, you are so funny."

"Do you want to watch TV or something?" Leah wasn't sure how eager Charity was to sample the world. She didn't want to offer her something she didn't feel comfortable doing.

"I do not think so," Charity said, eyeing the TV's blank screen. "I thought it would be fun to bake bread and cookies. You told me you wanted to do this sometime."

"This could turn into a real adventure."

Charity took inventory of Leah's staples and made a list, and together they went to the grocery store. With Charity in her car, her prayer cap tied securely under her chin so that the wind wouldn't blow it off, Leah was again struck by their differences. She couldn't imagine not being able to drive, to go wherever she pleased, whenever she wanted.

They bought supplies, returned to the apartment and went right to work. First they started the bread. "Because it must rise," Charity explained. Leah watched Charity sprinkle yeast into warm water, and after measuring out a few cups of flour, she eventually ended up with a soft mound of dough. Once it had risen to twice its size, Charity placed the lump on a floured countertop and began to knead it. Watching Charity's quick, sure motions made Leah feel like a klutz. "Now you try it." Charity turned the project over to Leah.

Leah jabbed at the lump. "It feels icky."

"You must work harder. It is dough, not glass."

Leah pounded the lump, and flour puffed into her face and hair. Charity burst into laughter. "You look like a snowman."

Leah giggled too. She folded the dough over and threw herself into kneading it. As she worked on the bread dough, Charity started making chocolate chip cookies. "Can I ask you something?" Leah said. "I know it's none of my business, but do you like Jonah?"

Charity stopped mixing the cookie dough. "I have ridden home from Sunday singing in his buggy many times."

"How about in his car?"

Color flooded Charity's face. "Do not tell anyone, please."

Taken aback by Charity's reaction, Leah said, "I won't. But what's the big deal? Buggy, car—it's still the same thing: You like Jonah."

"The buggy is acceptable. The car is not."

"You rode in my car."

"Cars are not approved by Papa, but it is better with you than with Jonah."

"He's never . . . you know . . . tried anything with you, has he?"

Charity turned wide, innocent eyes on Leah. "Do you mean, does he get fresh?"

"I guess that's what I mean."

"Jonah respects me. He would not shame me."

"I'm sorry. I didn't mean to embarrass you. It's just that he's acting English and you're still being Amish, so there's a gap between the two of you. I can tell he likes you, but I wondered how you felt. And I know how guys can be. I just don't want to see him take advantage of you." Leah didn't add that she didn't trust him.

"I have not had many experiences with boys, Leah, but Jonah is the boy I care for the most. We meet, but very carefully because my papa doesn't approve. Once Jonah is finished with his fling and returns to Amish life, then Papa will have no problem with our dating."

"When do you see him?"

"He comes to my house late at night when all are asleep. He shines a flashlight on my window. I make certain not to disturb Rebekah, and I go downstairs and meet with him. In the winter, we stay in the kitchen. In the summer, on the porch."

Leah stared openmouthed, unable to imagine sweet, dear Charity sneaking around behind her parents' backs. It seemed so out of character. "Then you've been seeing him for a long time?"

"Over a year."

"Wow, Charity. I never thought . . . I mean, I had no idea."

"We are special to each other. But it is a secret because we don't want to be teased, and because he is not ready yet to join the church."

"Are you telling me that he's the guy you want to marry?"

Charity squared her chin. "I am sixteen now and I want very much to be married. I want to have my own house, like my sister Sarah. Jonah is a good choice. Once he is baptized, he will ask Papa if he can marry me."

"I had no idea things were that serious between you two." Leah vowed to be nicer to Jonah. "Is this going to happen any time soon?"

Charity laughed. "It may be years before I marry. You must promise to come to my wedding."

"I'll try." Leah thought about her own future—where she was headed and what might be in store for her. Marriage seemed a scary choice. Until now, it hadn't worked for her mother. Leah certainly didn't want five passes at it to get it right for herself.

Charity broke into Leah's thoughts. "Let the bread rise again and help me with the cookies."

The bread looked thoroughly beaten, so Leah wrestled the globby mass into a couple of bread pans and covered it with a cloth as Charity directed. They set it aside again, scooped spoonfuls of the cookie dough onto cookie sheets and set the sheets in the oven. Soon the apartment was filled with the aroma of buttery chocolate.

When it was time to bake the bread, Leah removed the cloth. "Yikes! Look how fat it's gotten. Is it safe?"

"It is perfect. You are a good baker, Leah."

Leah's only memory of baking was from when she was a small child. She and her grandmother Hall had baked and decorated Christmas cookies one rainy afternoon.

The bread was tucked into the oven and the two of them had collapsed on the sofa to chow down on cookies and milk when Ethan returned. "Smells good," he said, glancing from one to the other.

"Want one? Plate's on the counter." Leah pointed.

He stood looking at the mound of dirty bowls, utensils and cookie sheets and at the sticky, floury countertops. He stared hard at both of the girls. "It looks like an explosion has happened. Were you hurt, Leah?"

Leah stood, glanced into a mirror and gasped. Flour streaked her clothing and hair. It was even stuck to her eyelashes. Chocolate smudged her nose. Charity looked neat and clean, without a speck of flour on her skin or dress. The three of them looked at each other. They began to giggle, then to laugh. "I look like I took a flour shower," Leah managed to say, which started them laughing all over again.

Ethan grabbed a sponge. "I will help," he said. He gently lifted Leah's chin and swiped the cool, damp sponge down her cheeks, along her chin and forehead, and then softly across her lips. Her laughter quieted as she gazed up at him. His expression was intense, his touch feather soft. Light from a window across the room slanted through the curtains, casting him in bronze, his hair in gold. Her mouth went suddenly dry. Her pulse pounded in her ears. Every nerve ending in her body tingled. She was only vaguely aware when Charity slipped out of the room. "Thank you for the cleanup," Leah told him.

He dropped the sponge and cradled her face between his palms. "You are welcome, Leah," he answered. "Believe me, it is my pleasure."

She rose on her tiptoes to accept a kiss from his warm, full, honey-colored mouth.

Leah kept postcards from her mother and Neil stuck to her refrigerator with colorful magnets. One had been mailed from the Los Angeles airport, several from Hawaii. Each held detailed descriptions of their vacation. The latest one read:

> Dear Leah,
> I wish you could see these islands. I never dreamed there could be so many flowers growing in the wild. Why, there's a garden right outside our bungalow door. By the time you get this, we'll have been on the boat for three

> days. I hope I don't embarrass Neil and throw up. I've been seasick before and it's no picnic. But I'm so happy! I know your doctor's appointment is coming up soon, so I'll be checking with you about it. I hope you are well and having a wonderful summer. I love you, Leah. I don't think I ever told you that enough when you were growing up. Forgive me my lapse.
>
> Love, Mother

Added was a postscript from Neil sending his love too.

In the same batch of mail, a letter arrived from Dr. Thomas, her orthopedic oncologist in Indianapolis, telling her that her appointment for testing and a checkup had been scheduled for the following Thursday.

The next day after work, Leah drove out to the farm. She went directly to the barn, where she thought Ethan might be working. She found him repairing tools. "What is it?" he asked when he saw her.

She told him about the upcoming appointment. "Did you mean what you said about coming with me?"

"I will come."

Just then Mr. Longacre came into the barn. He stopped short when he saw Leah talking to Ethan. "Good day." He greeted her without smiling.

"I—I was just leaving," Leah said self-consciously. No matter how many times she saw Ethan's father, she never grew accustomed to him. The man was not rude to her, but she felt his disapproval whenever she came around. She hurried out of the barn, pausing to catch her breath and slow her rapid heartbeat. Then she heard Ethan and his father talking in German.

She couldn't understand the words, but their exchange was loud and sounded angry. It ended with the noise of a slammed door. *My fault,* Leah told herself. She hurried to her car before anyone could catch her eavesdropping and sped away.

NINE

It rained the day Leah drove the hundred and twenty miles to Indianapolis. But she couldn't have cared less. With Ethan riding beside her, the day didn't seem one bit gloomy.

As she sped along the freeway, Ethan asked, "Are you nervous about the testing?"

"A little. I wish it was over. I hate hospitals. Don't you?"

"I'm not so sure. The only time I've been in one, I met you. This does not seem like such a bad thing to me. Without the hospital, how would we have ever known one another?"

He had a point there. "Okay, so I won't hate them so much anymore."

He watched as she passed a semitrailer. "You drive well."

"I like to drive. Honestly, if you ever want to get your license, I'll let you use my car to take the test."

"Papa would never approve."

To Leah, it seemed that there was very little Jacob Longacre approved of. "Jonah drives."

"I am not Jonah." He reached over and turned on the car radio, listening intently to several stations before settling on one that played country music.

"You rebel, but you don't really do anything too far out in left field," Leah said, shaking her head. "I don't understand you, Ethan. Why don't you go all the way? Like Jonah does?"

"I cannot," he said, turning his attention to the countryside passing outside the window.

Leah realized he was closing the subject. She warned herself not to pry. He would always be an enigma to her. In English clothes, he appeared to be a regular guy. But she knew her world was still foreign to him, and despite his testing of the English lifestyle, he was Amish at his core.

Once they arrived at the hospital, Leah went

to the X-ray department, filled out paperwork, and sat with Ethan in the adjacent waiting room. She was scheduled for both bone scans and MRIs of her leg and hand. Since the original X rays had shown that cancer had eaten away bones in these places, these were the areas the doctors were most concerned with. "The doctors make me feel like I'm parts of a puzzle," she told Ethan while they waited for her name to be called. "Like these few pieces of me are all that matter. Sometimes a doctor hardly even looks at my face. He just stares at my knee and finger as if they're separated from the rest of my body."

"But your face is so pretty. How could he not stare at you?"

Ethan always said things that touched her. She gave him a smile. "Have I ever told you how much I appreciate you?"

When it was Leah's turn, she squeezed Ethan's hand, took a deep breath and followed the technician into the X-ray room. The procedures took about an hour, and when both were over, she and Ethan went to another lab, where she filled out more paperwork and waited to have her blood drawn. "This is my least favorite part," she told Ethan. "During my chemo treatments, they were always sticking needles in me and testing my blood. I think they wanted to see if the chemo was helping me or killing me."

He looked alarmed. "The chemo could have harmed you?"

Hastily she added, "It's all right. Sometimes you have to take a little poison and kill off good cells along with the bad ones. The important thing is killing off the bad guys."

He seemed to understand her point. "In farming, it is the same. Some of the chemicals used to kill insects and blight can be harmful to healthy things. Once Rebekah's chickens got into rat poison and several died."

"I'll bet it broke her heart. I know how much she cares about those chickens."

"She never knew. When I found the dead ones, I quickly took them away, went to a neighbor's, and bought others to replace them."

Ethan's confession endeared him to Leah even more. Who else would have tried to protect his sister's sensitive heart so discreetly? "I think that was sweet and caring." To prove it, she kissed him on the cheek.

He pulled back, his eyes twinkling. "If I am to get such a reward for substituting chickens, I will tell you about every good deed I do."

"Don't push your luck."

"I probably did her no favor," he added thoughtfully.

"Why's that?"

"Death is part of the cycle of life, Leah. We learn that lesson very early on a farm. We see it in the changing of the seasons. We see it in the birthing of new calves. Only the strongest ones survive. We help all we can, but if it is too much expense, it is better to let the weak ones die."

His point of view surprised her. "You mean you allow money to decide whether or not a calf lives? That sounds kind of cruel."

"Feed is expensive, and a farm must be productive. It is the way of things."

"Good thing you don't feel that way about people."

"People are different. People have souls. Animals do not."

Leah thought about her dead father and grandmother. She still missed them and hoped their souls had found peace after death.

Once her testing was complete, Leah returned with Ethan to the floor where she'd spent so many days just before Christmas. As they rode the elevator up, Ethan asked, "Why do you want to visit this place? It is depressing you."

She wasn't sure herself. "I'll never really understand what happened to me here, Ethan. But *something* happened. I think I'm still trying to sort it all out."

"You had an extraordinary experience, that's for sure," Ethan told her. "But perhaps it is better not to think upon it too much."

Leah knew he was right, but she couldn't help herself. The days and nights she'd spent there; the fear she'd felt; the mysterious appearances by Gabriella, whom Leah had assumed was a nurse but who wasn't; finding the diary of Molly's dead sister—all came back to her in a rush. She couldn't let go of any part of the experience.

Leah and Ethan got off the elevator and went to the nurses' station. Nobody behind the desk looked familiar. She asked one of the nurses, "Is Molly Thrasher working today?"

"Molly's taking a patient down to the lab," the nurse explained.

"We must have just missed her down there," Leah told Ethan. Then she said to the nurse, "Would you please tell her that Leah Lewis-

Hall is here and that I'll be in the rec room for the next thirty minutes?"

Leah and Ethan walked down the hallway, stopping at the door of the room she and Rebekah had shared. Two young patients were in the beds, each watching TV. The room looked smaller than she remembered. She had no desire to go inside.

In the recreation room, in the corner where the magnificent tree had stood, children's art-work was taped to the wall. "I loved that Christmas tree your father brought," Leah said. "It was the prettiest tree I ever saw. When I couldn't sleep at night, I'd come down here just to look at it. And I'd imagine the woods where it came from."

"And now you have seen the woods with your own eyes."

"With you," she said, the memory of that night with him still bright.

Ethan slid his arm around her waist, and she snuggled against his side. "This seems a good time to ask you," he said. "My friends are hav-ing a party on the Fourth of July. Will you go with me?"

"Do you think it's a good idea? They tell

me I'm welcome, but sometimes I'm not so sure."

"They do not know you as well as I," Ethan said.

And they don't want to, either, Leah thought. She would always be English in their eyes. And she'd never forgotten what Kathy had told her that first day at work about the Amish sticking with their own kind. She said, "Tell me about the party."

"We will go to the county fair. After the late fireworks, there will be a camping party on the Yoder farm property. I would like to have you with me."

"Camping? You mean, like staying in tents outside all night?"

"The summer nights are warm. We will only use sleeping bags. It is something the group does every year. Even my father and his friends did it when they were growing up. I have not gone before, but this year I would like to go. But only if you will come with me."

"I'm having trouble imagining your father taking a fling," Leah said seriously.

"He is not such a stern man, Leah. But he does not bend easily. My father is an elder in the church and feels he must set an example for others."

"If you say so. Will Charity be at the campout?"

"Only if I go."

"So, in other words, if I don't go, neither of you will go." The invitation didn't seem as appealing cast in that light.

"I would not want to go if you do not come," he said. "Being with you is more important than being with my friends."

Now Leah felt she would be acting petty to care whether the others liked her or not. The important person was Ethan, and he wanted her with him. "I'd like to go," she told him. "I've never camped before, but I'd like to be with you too."

"Then it is settled. We will go to the fair on the Fourth of July, watch the fireworks, and spend the night camping with the others."

She gave him a smile that she hoped conveyed more enthusiasm than she felt.

Leah urged Ethan into the patient library that adjoined the rec room. It hadn't changed much. The books looked more dog-eared than ever, and someone had left the card catalog drawer open. She closed it and went to the shelf where she and Ethan had discovered Emily's diary.

She fingered the bindings, half expecting to see some reminder of Gabriella. There was none. Nothing at all to reflect that strange and wonderful night when the woman had come into her room, talked to her and touched her. "For a long time, the Gabriella mystery drove me crazy," she said to Ethan, her thoughts turning away from the July Fourth party. "I read everything I could about the supernatural. About ghosts. About angels."

"I do not believe in ghosts," Ethan said. "But I do believe in angels."

"Do you believe that each of us has a special guardian angel?" she asked.

He looked thoughtful. "I am not sure about that. You ask so many questions, Leah. Do you believe in angels or not?"

"I do now," Leah answered emphatically. "Did you know that a lot of people think that when they die they will turn into angels?"

Ethan looked at her and said, "I saw it in a movie, when I first began to try English things. It was a story about a person who dies and comes back as an angel so that he can make up for bad things he did to people while he was alive." He shook his head. "I knew it was not true. People get new bodies in heaven, but they do not turn into angels. Angels are separate beings from people."

Leah continued to tell him what she'd learned in her reading. "I read about people who were miraculously healed. Or rescued. Some unexplainable things have happened to people—like what happened to me."

"Why do you need an explanation? Can't you just accept the gift you've been given?" Ethan toyed with the ends of her hair, curling long strands around his finger.

"I guess I'll have to. But I still can't help wondering, why me?"

Just then the door opened, and they turned to see Molly.

"How are you?" Molly asked excitedly. "I sort of had a premonition that I'd be seeing you soon." She gave Leah a hug.

"I think I'm doing fine, but Dr. Thomas hasn't checked me over yet."

Molly turned toward Ethan, smiled pleasantly, then asked, "So, Leah, aren't you going to introduce me to your friend?"

TEN

Leah and Ethan exchanged glances. Ethan said, "I am Ethan Longacre."

"I—I didn't recognize you," Molly stammered. "I'm sorry." Leah realized that Molly had never seen Ethan dressed English-style before.

"It is all right," he said. "I guess I do look different to you."

"But very good," she added quickly. "How's your sister Rebekah doing?"

"She is well. Recovered from her spider bite."

"Good. She is such a sweet little girl." Molly looked at Leah. "I'm so glad you stopped by to see me. I've thought of you a hundred times since you were here. Come, sit." They pulled out chairs at the reading table, Molly on one side, Leah and Ethan on the other. "Tell me, what are you doing this summer?"

Leah told Molly about her summer job and living arrangements.

"Your own apartment," Molly said, obviously impressed. "I was twenty-two before I had my own place. Then I got married and had kids, and I may never have the place to myself again."

The three of them laughed. Leah said, "Tell us about Christmas at your parents', and about reading Emily's diary."

"It was a very special time," Molly said, folding her hands on the table. "Imagine hearing someone speak to you from the grave. That's how we all felt as we read Emily's entries. It was as if she were in the room with us, looking over our shoulders. It brought back a hundred memories . . . good memories. She was a wonderful girl who died before she should have. I've been looking into having her diary published." Molly glanced from Ethan to Leah. "I think her insights, her feelings about her cancer and what she was going through, would be a help to kids today."

Leah nodded slowly. "Probably so. I know I

sure would have liked to read something by a person my age when I was told I had cancer. You feel so alone. If it hadn't been for you, and Ethan and his sisters, it would have been a whole lot harder."

"Thank you," Molly said. "Medical procedures may change over time, but human emotions don't. Being told you have a disease must be some of the hardest news in the world to hear. Especially when you're young, like Emily was. Her diary was really clear about how isolated and lonely she felt."

"Getting her diary published is a good idea," Ethan said. "I hope you have good luck."

"Thanks. And I haven't forgotten the role that strange woman Gabriella played in all this. I never have been able to figure out how she came to have my sister's diary." Molly leaned back in the chair. "Have you ever seen her again?"

"No. And neither has Rebekah, because I asked her."

"Well, unless she surfaces again, I'll never know. I guess that's not what's important anyway. The fact is, I have Emily's diary. I'll always be grateful for that."

Leah glanced at her watch. "I guess we

should be going. I don't want to keep Dr. Thomas waiting."

They stood, and at the door, Leah hugged Molly goodbye. "It was sure nice seeing you again."

"You too," said the nurse. "Anytime you're here, please stop by." She looked at Ethan and said, "That goes for you too. By the way, I like you in those clothes."

Ethan's face reddened, but Leah could tell he was pleased by Molly's comment.

When they reached Dr. Thomas's office, the receptionist ushered them into an exam room. The doctor entered, shook Ethan's hand, then placed the newest set of Leah's X rays on the light board. He said, "Your X rays look good. Any complaints?"

Leah licked her lips nervously. She told him about how her knee sometimes ached after work. He examined her knee, massaging the kneecap while studying the X rays. "I do see some inflammation."

Leah braced herself for bad news.

Dr. Thomas continued. "Such swelling is common among athletes when they strain their knees or elbows. Have you been bending a lot? Playing a sport before properly warming up?"

She told him about her job.

"That could explain it. I'll give you a cortisone injection at the site. If you keep having trouble, let me know. Take it easy for a few days and give it time to heal, all right?"

"All right." Leah didn't want a shot in her knee, but she'd been afraid it was more serious.

Dr. Thomas left and returned with a syringe. Leah gritted her teeth as he slid the needle into her knee. She saw Ethan turn his head. When the ordeal was over, she asked, "Am I cured? From the cancer, I mean."

Dr. Thomas put his hand on her shoulder. "Now, Leah, you know I can't say this soon after your treatment. You just completed chemo a few months ago."

"But you told me that the dark spots had started to shrink even before I started chemo."

"That is true," Dr. Thomas said. "And I have no medical explanation for it. But cancer is still a mystery in many ways. The more we find out about it, the more we realize we don't know." He removed the X-ray films from the light board. "My job is to keep watch over you. I want to see you again in the fall, so stop at my receptionist's desk and she'll make another appointment for you."

Leah got off the exam table. It wasn't the answer she had wanted, but for now it would have to do.

The doctor smiled. "I think your prognosis is very good, Leah. But remember, with cancer, it's one day at a time."

In the elevator, Leah sagged against the wall. "I'm glad that's over with."

"I can tell you are not happy with his words," Ethan said.

Leah felt tears of frustration building behind her eyes. "I guess I wanted him to tell me I was completely cured and he didn't ever want to see me again. I hate thinking every little ache and pain might be cancer returning."

Ethan ran his knuckles softly along her cheek. "You want to believe in a miracle, but you cannot. But that is what faith is, Leah. Believing in what we cannot see."

She sniffed hard. "You're right. I need more faith. And right this minute, I'm tired of talking about it and thinking about it."

"You were very brave when he gave you the shot," Ethan said. "You need a reward. I know, I will buy you supper and a present."

Leah fumbled for a tissue and dabbed at her eyes. "What kind of present?"

"Something to make you happy again. Something to make you smile for me."

They drove to a gigantic mall in one of the city's suburbs. The parking lot was crammed with cars; inside the mall, summer sales were announced by colorful signs decorated in red, white and blue. Flags sprouted out of merchandise displays. Aisles were thick with shoppers. Leah watched Ethan's reaction to the stores, crowds, and noise—a far cry from the sleepy little town of Nappanee.

They walked through the mall, stopping in front of store windows whenever something caught Ethan's eye. "Why are there so many stores selling clothes?" he asked.

"People like to buy clothes. It's fun."

He looked at her blankly. "I see that a person needs summer clothes and clothes for winter, but this is practical. In winter it is cold. In summer, hot. The same clothes will not do for both."

"People like to have clothes for lots of different things." Leah's closet was packed with clothes and she always thought she needed more. She added, "Plus, styles change. You can't wear the same old things year after year."

He made a face. "You are right. That would be horrible."

She punched him playfully.

By now they were walking through one of the better department stores. Ethan stopped short in front of a rack of swimsuits. His eyes grew large as he looked at an assortment of bikinis.

"Something wrong?" Leah asked.

"Do girls wear such things out in public?"

Leah was trying hard not to giggle at the expression on his face. "Only girls with great bodies," she said, holding one up. It was red, speckled with white stars. "Kind of patriotic, don't you think?"

He gulped. His gaze fell on the price tag. "We could feed a dairy cow for months on that much money."

Leah dangled the suit in front of her. "Well, I certainly don't want to cheat a poor cow out of her food."

Ethan's gaze flew to Leah's face. "You would not wear such a thing, would you?"

"There's nothing wrong with wearing a bikini," she said defensively. "And yes, I've worn one. I guess you've never lain on a beach and sunbathed, have you?"

"Is that why girls wear them? To get a suntan?"

Leah started to tell him that bikinis were fashion items in today's world. She also knew that tanning had never been the main reason she and her friends had worn bikinis. Boys noticed them in bikinis. She didn't want to admit that to Ethan. Feeling irritated, she hung the suit back on the rack. "I'm sorry, Ethan. I was teasing you, and I shouldn't have."

He stepped out of the main aisle and the flow of foot traffic. "You do not have to apologize," he said. "And I did not mean to sound so disapproving. But I believe that a woman's body should only be shared with her husband. She should not show it off to other men." He averted his eyes. "And I will also tell you that it bothers me to think that other boys look at your body."

"You're jealous?"

He pondered her question before answering. "No. Jealousy is wrong. It serves no good, so I am not jealous. But it *does* hurt my heart to think about sharing you with others. You are beautiful, Leah. I hope you will not wear bikinis, but I would never tell you what to do."

With his words, Leah felt her irritation dissolve. "I know we're coming from different places, Ethan. And I know it's hard for you to understand this crazy modern world. I guess I don't give much thought to it myself—maybe I should. Just please remember, I really do respect your values. And I don't want you to think badly of me just because we don't see eye to eye on something like clothes."

Ethan raised his eyes, and a smile softened his face. "Many of my friends tell me I am too old-fashioned. I am trying to 'lighten up.' "

"I'll cut you some slack then," she said, taking his hand. "And you needn't worry about me parading around in a bikini. I won't do that either. If I'm going to spend this much money, I'd rather buy something that covers a lot more territory!"

Ethan laughed hard. "Oh, Leah, you are very funny."

It was good to hear him laugh. But Leah felt troubled. No matter how much time they spent together, it still seemed as if they were worlds apart. She had thought that over time, they might grow closer in the way that each of them viewed the world and how to live in it. At the moment, she wasn't sure if that would or could ever happen.

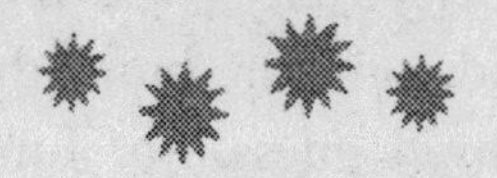

ELEVEN

After grabbing a hamburger in the food court, Leah and Ethan returned to cruising the mall. Ethan stopped in front of a large toy store. "Let's go in here," he said.

Leah hadn't been into a toy store for years, but she found walking through the aisles with Ethan fascinating. His gaze darted everywhere, absorbing the array of toys and playthings like a sponge soaking up water. He stopped by a model train display. He bent down, examining from every angle the perfect replica of an old-fashioned steam engine, tracks, countryside and miniature town.

"Cool, isn't it?" Leah asked.

"Yes," he answered.

"It runs on electricity," she reminded him.

"Why would someone build this?"

"For a hobby, I guess. For fun."

He shook his head. "This person has too much spare time."

Leah didn't want to get into another discussion with him about what was and wasn't practical. She wandered off and started sorting through a table filled with marked-down items. She picked up a bright pink plastic egg left over from the store's Easter merchandise. When she pushed a button on the side of the egg, the top half popped open and a small, fuzzy chick popped up and made a peeping noise.

"Ethan, look." Leah took it over to him for a demonstration. "Isn't this cute? I'd like to buy this for Rebekah. Do you think she'll like it?"

"She has real chickens."

"So what? This is really cute. And girls like cute little things."

"But what is the purpose of this toy?"

"Purpose! Does everything have to have a purpose for you? Can't you—" Leah was just warming up when she realized that he was teasing her. "I should slug you," she said.

He threw up his hands in mock surrender. "I would rather have a kiss."

She stalked to the counter and bought the plastic egg.

Out in the mall again, Leah paused at a store window and pointed. "Here's a hair salon. Were you serious about getting a different haircut?"

Ethan craned his neck to peer past posters for hair products. "I see only women in there."

"The salon is unisex. For both men and women," she explained. "We could talk to a stylist. Look through some books. Then you could decide."

He licked his lips nervously. "No one will laugh at me?"

"No way. It's their business to make people happy with their haircuts."

"We could talk to one . . . ," he said hesitantly.

Leah caught his arm. "It might cost some money. I mean, more than you think it's worth."

"I have money."

"Then let's go talk to them."

An hour later, Ethan's thick blond hair had been washed, cut and dried into a sleek new style. It was still conservative, but it looked modern, not home-done, like his original cut. His expression throughout the process was one of stoic resignation. He never even closed his eyes during the shampoo portion. "Relax," the stylist told him.

But when it was over and he saw himself in the mirror, Leah saw a grin creep out around the corners of his mouth. She thought he'd never looked more handsome, but she knew flattery would only embarrass him. Once they were out in the mall, she said, "I like it. Do you?"

"Yes. But back home, I will be teased by my friends."

"If they don't have anything better to do than tease you about a haircut, then tell them to get a life."

Ethan grinned. "I will tell them."

Leah looked at her watch. "It's almost nine. I think we'd better start back."

In the car, Ethan said, "Today was fun, Leah. I liked being with you. I liked the adventure."

She thought it odd that he'd consider a visit to a hospital and a mall adventurous. Then she reconsidered. He'd probably never spent a whole day doing things that didn't revolve around his family or farmwork. The Amish probably thought that shopping without a specific purpose was frivolous. "Anytime you want another adventure, tell me," Leah said. "I liked being with you today too."

It was after midnight when they turned onto the Longacre property. "Stop the car here," Ethan said. "I will walk the rest of the way to the house."

Leah turned off the engine. "Good thinking. We don't want to wake anybody up." She asked, "You won't get in trouble, will you? With your father, I mean." She hadn't forgotten their raised voices the day she'd stopped by to tell Ethan about her doctor's appointment.

"If you are asking if Papa is angry at me for leaving today, the answer is yes."

Leah winced. "I'm sorry. I didn't mean to make him mad at you." She played with her fingers in the dark. "I know he doesn't like me."

"That is not true. He has not forgotten your kindness to Rebekah when you were in the hospital together."

"Okay, so he tolerates me. But he doesn't like your hanging around with me."

"He has reasons," Ethan said, not bothering to deny that Leah's observation was correct.

"Such as?"

Ethan didn't answer, and the silence stretched into a long, awkward minute. "I cannot say. But it is not *you* as a person, Leah."

His refusal to tell her was infuriating. Still, she was determined not to nag him. "Look, I know you get up at five-thirty. And I've got to go to work in the morning also."

"Leah, I am not keeping a secret to make you angry, or because I do not care about you," he said, as though sensing her feelings.

"You don't owe me any explanations, Ethan. I am English and you are not. I guess in your father's mind, that's reason enough." She started the engine. "I hope you don't catch too much flak about your hair."

Ethan opened the car door and stepped out into the weak pool of light cast by the car's interior lights. "Wait," he said, before she could pull away. He reached into his shirt pocket and pulled out a small package. "This is for you. I told you I was going to buy you a present."

"When did you buy it? We were together the whole day."

"That is a secret. Open it."

She took a small box from the bag. In the box, nestled in cotton, was a porcelain lop-eared rabbit, not more than a few inches long. It glowed alabaster white in the light from the dashboard. "Oh, Ethan. It's beautiful."

"It is small. It is cute. You said girls like such things."

Leah realized that she couldn't hold a grudge against Ethan. Her annoyance with him evaporated. "You're a very thoughtful, kind person, Ethan. Thank you—not just for the present, but for going with me today. It meant a lot to me."

"You are welcome. You make me happy, Leah. Happier than anything else I have ever known."

Leah watched him walk toward the old farmhouse and back into his Amish world. She drove off, to return to hers.

The next day, Mrs. Stoltz asked Leah to go out to the Longacre farm to buy fresh vegetables for her kitchen. "They have the best in the whole area," she told Leah, "and I know you're friends with them."

Leah figured Kathy must have said something to Mrs. Stoltz about Leah's knowing the Longacres. She was happy to have an excuse to see her friends.

"I like Ethan's haircut," Charity said as she and Leah walked in the garden, picking ripe vegetables. Colorful flowers, used as natural insect repellants, grew between the orderly rows. "Everyone noticed it then, I guess."

"Yes. It was noticed."

"Did your family approve?"

"Rebekah and I approved."

"But your parents didn't?"

"Not Papa. He told Ethan that he looked fancy."

Knowing her fears had been realized, Leah asked, "What did Ethan say?"

"He told Papa that it was his hair and that he could do with it as he liked."

"You mean they argued about it." Leah couldn't understand what was so bad about Ethan's getting his hair cut differently. He'd done nothing wrong.

"Not an argument," Charity said, answering Leah's question. "Papa does not argue. But you know when he is not pleased."

"I'll bet," Leah muttered. She couldn't accept Mr. Longacre's stern ways.

Charity lifted the stalk of a tomato plant, plucked several rosy red ripe ones, and put them in the basket she carried. "Let's not talk of Ethan's haircut," she said. "Let's talk about the carnival and campout. Ethan says that you will come with us."

"It sounds like fun." Leah hoped she sounded sincere.

"I am excited. It is something we all look forward to while we are growing up. This is my first year to be old enough to go."

"Will you go with Jonah?"

Charity had been pulling green beans from climbing vines. At the mention of Jonah, her hands grew still. "Yes. But no one knows except you."

"Don't you think kids will figure it out when they see the two of you together? Why keep it such a big secret?"

"We go as a group, not as couples," Charity said. "Jonah will be there. I will be there. That is all."

"But you and Jonah know that the two of you are really together, right?"

"That is right."

Leah couldn't fathom this logic, but she knew it was important to Charity to pretend that she and Jonah were just part of the group, nothing more. "I won't tell a soul," she said.

Charity handed the basket to Leah, gathered the corners of her apron to make a bowl, and tossed a handful of green beans into it. "I have a favor to ask of you, Leah."

"Sure. Just name it."

"I want you to help me change my appearance for the campout."

"Like how?"

"I want to dress English for that night."

Warning bells went off in Leah's head. "Why can't the other Amish girls help you?"

"I could ask some of them, but I don't want to. I want you to help me. You are real English. They are not."

"I've seen some of them dressed up, and they look pretty real to me." It wasn't that Leah didn't want to help Charity—she did. It was that she didn't want to get into any more hot water with Mr. Longacre. She was afraid he might forbid Charity and Ethan to see her anymore. Leah knew that would make her miserable.

"Also," Charity continued, "I cannot buy any different clothes. I will have to borrow them. And I have seen how many beautiful clothes you have. I was hoping you would let me borrow some for that night. Because it means so much to me to look pretty."

Leah felt boxed in. But she knew she wouldn't refuse Charity. "Sure. If that's what you want."

Charity's face broke into a bright smile. "Oh, Leah, thank you. I knew you would help me. You are a true friend."

Leah hoped she was doing the right thing. "What if your parents find out?"

"Who would tell them?"

Leah could think of several who might let it slip—not to hurt Charity, but to hurt Leah. Still, she'd already said she would help. "Have Ethan bring you by my place this weekend. We can go through my closet and try on some stuff. See what you like. And what looks good on you."

"Yes. Yes," Charity said. "And makeup too."

Leah took a deep breath. "Sure. And makeup too."

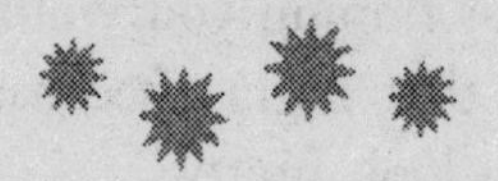

TWELVE

On Saturday, Ethan brought Charity over to Leah's apartment. When Ethan had left to do errands, Leah and Charity sorted through Leah's closet. "I left most of my stuff back home," Leah said, tossing pieces of clothing onto the bed. "And with working every day, shopping hasn't been high on my priority list."

Charity only stared wide-eyed at the heaps of tops, shorts, skirts and slacks.

"Oh, this is cute," Leah said, holding up a colorful striped T-shirt and matching shorts. "Try it on."

"I do not think I would feel comfortable in shorts," Charity said.

"What am I saying? Of course you wouldn't. How about this?" Leah held up a pair of white jeans.

"I don't know." Charity fingered the material.

"Try them on."

Charity slipped into the bathroom to change.

"You look great," Leah said when her friend emerged.

"They are tight."

"But you have a cute figure. They look good on you."

Charity viewed her backside in the full-length mirror hanging on the bedroom door. "This is not the way I wish for everyone to see my bottom."

Leah giggled. "All right. We'll try something else."

Eventually Charity settled on a long, colorful peasant skirt and a cotton top. Leah even owned a pair of sandals that matched the outfit and fit Charity. "This is perfect," Charity said after spinning in front of the mirror.

Leah leaned back on her elbows on the bed. "You look terrific."

Charity's eyes sparkled. "I did not want to

wear plain jeans like so many of the other girls will wear. I want to look different. Special."

Leah jumped up. "Time for hair and makeup."

Leah sat Charity on a chair, took down her thick hair from the bun at the nape of her neck and brushed it out. "How about a French braid?" She worked quickly, then tied the end with a red ribbon. Next she artfully applied blush, powder, mascara and pink lip gloss to Charity's smooth skin.

"What do you think?" Leah stepped back and let Charity see herself.

Charity stared at her image. "I can hardly believe it's me."

"It's you, all right."

"My friends won't know me."

"I thought that was the point."

Charity turned to look at Leah. "Will you help me dress on the night of the fair?"

"Sure. Now it's time for you to help me," Leah said. "I don't have a sleeping bag. And I don't know what's expected of me on this campout."

"Ethan and I will bring you a sleeping bag. We own several. As for the party, here's what I know about it. After the fair, we will all ride over to the Yoder farm and build a campfire. Everyone will bring food to cook and share. The sleeping bags are for those who wish to sleep. But few sleep. Most stay up all night."

"What should I cook?"

"I will bring enough for both of us. My sister Sarah has told me that mostly everyone eats, talks, visits. Some will bring radios, so we will dance. In the morning, we will remake the fire and eat again. It will be wonderful fun. You will see."

Leah had attended many sleepovers before, but never a coed one. She thought it ironic that her first all-nighter with guys and girls together would be with the Amish. "You know," she said, "except for you and Ethan, I don't have any friends in your group."

Charity tapped her finger against her chin. "I did not think of that." She flashed Leah an innocent smile. "But once they get to know you, they will like you as much as I do."

Leah didn't want to burst her friend's bubble, but she didn't have any of the confidence Charity did. Charity was too caught up in her own happiness to think about Martha. Leah wasn't.

Leah had no illusions that the Amish girls would welcome her with open arms. None at all.

Leah was amazed by the number of tourists who began to pour into town for the July Fourth holiday. They came to Amish Acres, a hundred-year-old Amish homestead where the Amish lifestyle was perfectly preserved. Demonstrations of spinning, weaving and quilting took place daily. There was a large restaurant specializing in simple but abundant Amish cooking, and a gift shop filled with Amish wares that attracted carloads of sightseers. Charity's oma had several quilts on display in the shop, as well as jars of jelly and pumpkin butter. A unique round, wooden, barnlike theater on the Acres showcased plays several days a week.

The bed-and-breakfast was full, and Leah and Kathy both worked long hours. They were changing beds together one morning when Leah asked, "Is it always like this on holidays?"

"Pretty much," Kathy said. "I'm glad I'm leaving for camp next week."

Leah realized she was going to miss Kathy. Not only because she worked hard, but because Kathy was friendly and talkative. They didn't socialize outside work, but that was because Kathy had a steady boyfriend and Leah spent whatever time she could with Ethan. "How can you go off and leave me?" Leah wailed.

"Mrs. Stoltz will hire someone else, or she already has, I guess. She knew my schedule." Kathy grinned. "And don't forget, you *wanted* to spend the summer here."

"I hadn't expected to be tripping over bodies, though. Tourists are clogging the streets."

"Tourists are a fact of life."

"The Amish don't like them very much. Not that I blame them. Tourists are always in their face, trying to take their pictures when they know the Amish don't like it. Mr. Longacre posted a No Trespassing sign on his property because a carload of tourists drove up to his house one afternoon just to look the place over. They acted insulted when he didn't invite them inside. Can you imagine people being so inconsiderate and insensitive?"

Kathy fluffed two pillows and tossed one to Leah. "Don't feel too sorry for the Amish," she said. "Sure they hate the commotion tourists cause, but they like the extra income they bring in. They tolerate the tourists because it's money in their pockets."

Leah thought Kathy's assessment harsh. She'd seen the large produce stand on the side of the highway, at the edge of the Longacre property, that the Amish community had built. There the abundance of produce, fruit, eggs, jellies, breads and other goods from surrounding Amish farms was sold. The stand was almost overwhelmed with customers. Rebekah was part of the group of younger kids and teenagers who helped out there. "There's nothing wrong with taking advantage of a bad situation," Leah said defensively.

Kathy shrugged. "The one thing the Amish really have to worry about with so many tourists around is getting run over. Those buggies are so slow, and tourists are always plowing into them."

"Really?" Leah herself had gotten stuck in traffic behind a poky Amish buggy, and she remembered Simeon on his skates.

"It happens all the time. Horses and buggies are no match for cars. Someone's always getting maimed. Or worse."

Leah grimaced. "I can see why they hate tourist season."

"One good thing about being Amish, though, is that they take care of their own. Whenever a disaster happens, the whole clan rallies to help out. Farmwork gets done, animals get taken care of—I do admire them for that." Kathy shook out fresh towels for the bathroom. "But for the most part, I think the Amish are old-fashioned and stubborn. What's the difference between riding in a car and driving one yourself?"

Leah had often thought the same thing, but she didn't want to admit it to Kathy. "Look at the time," she said suddenly. "I told Mrs. Stoltz I'd go buy fresh salad makings for the lunch crowd. I'd better get it done."

Leah drove directly to the Amish produce stand. When she pulled up, Rebekah came running over. "Leah, I've sold six dozen eggs today," the little girl said with a big grin. Her front tooth was partially grown in, making her look especially cute.

"Good for you!"

"Are you going to the fair tomorrow night to see the fireworks?" Rebekah asked.

"Yes. Are you going?" Leah thought it best not to mention that she was going with Ethan and Charity.

"Mama and Papa are taking me. Maybe we'll see you."

Leah wondered what would happen if Charity's parents ran into them. Especially with Charity dressed English. "Maybe." Leah tugged playfully on one of Rebekah's braids. "How's my chicken doing?"

"She's getting very big. I think she will lay many eggs."

"I sure hope so. I don't want a lazy chicken. Is Charity at the house?" Leah asked.

"She's working in the apple orchard with Mama and Oma today. But you can go visit her if you want."

Leah bought the produce she needed and put it in her car. She wanted to talk about the next night's plans and decided to take a chance on going up to the house, hoping Mr. Longacre wouldn't spot her. In the distance she saw Ethan working in a field of corn and started walking toward him. On foot, she figured, she'd be less noticeable than in her car.

When he saw her coming, he came over to

the fence to meet her. "Leah! I have been thinking about you."

His admission pleased her. "Same here," she said. "The corn looks like it's growing. When I first came, it was barely out of the ground."

"There is a saying that it will be a good harvest if the corn is knee-high by July Fourth." Ethan mopped his forehead with a handkerchief.

"It looks fine to me."

"*You* look fine to *me*."

"Glad you noticed."

"I always notice you, Leah."

Her heartbeat quickened. "How do you want to handle going to the fair tomorrow night? Should I drive?"

"My family will leave for the fair after lunch. Oma and Opa will also be going. No one will be at home. Come to the house before suppertime."

"What if they run into us at the fair?"

"The fair is very large, and hundreds of people will be there. It is unlikely."

"I just don't want them to think I'm a bad influence on Charity."

Ethan took her hand. "Charity has made this choice. She would do it with or without you."

"If you say so." Still, Leah didn't feel totally absolved. What they were doing was sneaky.

Ethan lifted her chin. "We will have a very good time tomorrow night. You will see. All will be well."

Leah wanted to believe him because it was so important. He wanted his friends to accept her. She wanted it too. But Jonah had essentially told her that English and Amish didn't mix. And everything she'd seen so far this summer—the tourists, their loud voices, their inconsiderate actions—told her that was the truth. Leah was English. Ethan, his family and his friends were not. She tried hard to be respectful and tolerant of their Amish customs. But nothing could change the reality of their differences. Nothing.

THIRTEEN

Leah arrived at the farm the next day in the late afternoon. She carried in a sack full of clothes for Charity, and while she helped her dress and put on makeup, Ethan loaded the car with sleeping bags, a cooler and containers of food. He was sitting in the parlor when Leah and Charity came down the stairs. He jumped to his feet.

Charity twirled in front of him. "What do you think?"

"I think you look very pretty."

Leah could see by Charity's smile that her brother's compliment mattered to her. "Then you approve?" Leah asked.

Ethan's gaze found hers. "I approve."

They drove the several miles to the county fairgrounds with the convertible's top down. The weather was typical for July—hot and sticky. At the fair, they parked in a field crammed with other cars and walked to the admission gate. After paying, Ethan said, "We are to meet the others in the carnival area." He took Leah's hand, and the three of them threaded their way through the throngs of people.

The carnival arcade consisted of games of chance and rides and even more people waiting in long lines. At the Ferris wheel, Leah saw Jonah scanning the crowd anxiously. When Jonah saw Charity, his eyes widened, and then a grin split his face. "I like what I see," he told her when the three of them were standing in front of him.

"Leah helped me," Charity said.

Jonah glanced at Leah. "Leah has only magnified what God has already created."

"Where to now?" Leah asked.

"I will win you a teddy bear," Ethan said.

They went over to a booth where a barker was urging people to try their skill at knocking over a stack of wooden bottles with a baseball. "Win the little lady a prize!" the man shouted. "Three tries for a dollar."

Ethan slapped down a dollar bill. "I will try."

The barker grinned. "Here you go, son. Dump 'em and your girl gets her pick of prizes."

Leah leaned over and whispered into Ethan's ear. "These things are rigged. You shouldn't waste your money."

"It is only a dollar," Ethan said. "And I may get lucky." He picked up the balls and threw them in quick succession, knocking down the bottles.

Leah didn't know who was more surprised, she or the barker. The man gave Ethan a sour smile. "You did it, kid. What does the lady want?"

Leah picked out a bear, and Ethan tucked it under his arm. "How'd you do that?" she asked once they had walked away.

Ethan flashed her a sly smile. "These people think because we are Amish we are slow or dumb. I learned long ago just how to throw the ball to beat them. They are always surprised when I win."

"And who taught you how to beat them?"

He stiffened. "Someone from long ago. It is not important."

His answer mystified Leah. He was shutting

her out again from something in his past. Determined not to let it bother her, she looped her arm through his. "You're just full of surprises, Ethan Longacre. And I like surprises."

His momentary moodiness vanished with a quick smile. "I like surprises too."

Jonah won Charity a stuffed toy at the next booth. Soon the four of them had their arms loaded with stuffed animals and inexpensive dolls and toys. "What are we going to do with all this stuff?" Leah asked.

"We will leave it with friends in one of the food booths," Ethan said. "The Yoders have a concession stand."

They left their prizes with the Yoders—all except for Leah's bear, which she insisted on carrying. When they returned to the carnival area, Leah recognized some of Jonah's friends standing near the roller coaster. They were talking, even flirting, with girls who weren't Amish. She wasn't sure why that bothered her, but it did. English girls—girls like her—seemed good enough to have fun with, but not good enough to date or take home to the family. Still, she was polite when introduced to the newcomers.

Within an hour, the group had ridden the

roller coaster, the bumper cars and the merry-go-round. Dusk was falling by the time Leah and Ethan got on the Ferris wheel. "Soon the fireworks will start over by the lake," Ethan said as the wheel began its slow ascent.

Leah saw the grayish blue water from the high vantage point. People were already gathered along the shore in lawn chairs and on blankets. "It already looks packed."

"Don't worry. Some of our friends are there saving places."

Since Leah hadn't yet run into Martha, she wondered if Jonah's sister was one of the friends saving places.

Their seat on the Ferris wheel swung to the very top, then lurched to a stop. Far below, Leah saw a man fiddling with the machinery. "We may have to watch from up here," she said, huddling closer to Ethan. "It sure is a long way down."

"Are you frightened? I have seen you drive. How could this be scary?"

She punched his arm good-naturedly. "Swinging in an open basket fifty feet in the air with nothing but a bar across my lap doesn't bother me one bit."

He laughed. "I like this ride best of all. It lets me see the earth as birds see it. As angels see it. Sometimes I dream that I am flying above the ground, swooping and soaring. I don't like waking up from that dream."

"You've never flown in an airplane, have you?"

He shook his head, but she saw a wistful look cross his face. "I would like to do that someday."

"You ought to see the clouds from the top side. They look like big fat cotton balls. Do you think angels play in the clouds?"

"Angels go anywhere they want." He brushed her hair with his lips. "Even on Ferris wheels at county fairs."

Leah felt as if she were melting. Ethan could say the sweetest things.

After the ride, they headed toward the lake. They searched the throngs for their friends. Charity was the first to spot them. "Over there." She waved at a group of about thirty kids lounging on quilts and blankets.

Leah settled next to Ethan, mindful of the glances from the group. She was the only non-Amish person among them. From the corner of her eye, she saw Martha. Martha kept glancing at Ethan covertly, and Leah knew that if it hadn't been for her, Martha undoubtedly would have been the one with Ethan tonight. Leah shifted so that Martha was completely out of her line of vision.

With a loud pop, the first volley of fireworks lit the sky. Cascades of color and showers of gold rained down in long streamers. Using her stuffed bear as a pillow, Leah stretched out. Ethan lay beside her and together they watched the brilliant lights dance overhead. With every burst, Leah felt Ethan's hand tighten on hers. Waves of contentment washed over her. She couldn't imagine anyplace else in the world she'd rather be than under a July Fourth fireworks display with Ethan.

Ethan asked, "Do you think your mother is seeing fireworks in the South Pacific?"

"According to Mom, a person can see a million stars out there. Who needs fireworks?" Her mother had called a few days before to hear how Leah's doctor's appointment had gone. Leah had given her mother a good report, not even mentioning her sore knee. The cortisone shot had helped immensely, but her bout with cancer seemed always to be lurking on the fringes of her mind.

Ethan sighed. "Sometimes I think about traveling all over the world."

Leah understood his longing. But for her, what he had—home and a sense of belonging—seemed more satisfactory than sailing the ocean. "Maybe someday you will," she said.

"It does not seem likely. But I wish I could."

When the fireworks show was over, the quilts were folded and the whole group joined the exodus of people headed home. The Amish kids were going to the Yoder farm for the campout. And Leah would be with them. She hoped she didn't do anything to embarrass herself. And she hoped that she and Ethan could hold on to the feelings they had for each other—regardless of all their differences.

A stream ran through the part of the farm where the campsite was set up. A large bonfire was built and blankets spread on the ground around it. Radios, portable CD players, picnic baskets and coolers were strewn around the blankets. A keg of beer sat in the sluggish stream. Leah was certain Jonah had sneaked it in. Leah noted that this night everyone had come in cars—not in buggies. And no one was dressed Amish.

She and Ethan settled on a quilt with Charity and Jonah. Jonah headed straight for the beer keg. Ethan pulled a package of hot dogs from their cooler. "Want one?"

"Sure," Leah said.

He handed her a piece of wire and stuck a hot dog on the end. They walked closer to the fire and began cooking the hot dogs. By the time they returned to the blanket, Charity had gone to talk to other friends, and Jonah had made several more trips to the keg.

Leah and Ethan sat on the blanket, scooped potato salad onto plates and began eating. Jonah came up and held out a plastic cup full of beer. "Want a drink, Ethan?"

"This is not a place for drinking, Jonah," Ethan responded. "You should not have brought this."

"You don't like my beer?" Jonah asked. His tone sounded challenging.

"No. I do not want your beer," he said evenly.

"Why do you not want to be with your

friends, Ethan?" Jonah asked. He swayed slightly. "Why are you letting your girlfriend make your decisions for you?"

Leah held her breath, waiting for Ethan's reaction.

Ethan stood. "I make my own choices, Jonah. And I do not choose to drink your beer."

Leah watched Ethan stoop over and rummage through the cooler and pull out two soda cans. He popped the tabs, handed one to Leah, and sat back down. To Jonah, Ethan said, "Why don't you eat something? We have salads. We have cakes."

"I don't want anything to eat. I want to talk to you about the way you treat your friends." He cast Leah a hard look. "Ever since she came into your life, you have no time for us. For your own kind."

"You are talking crazy," Ethan said.

In the light from the bonfire, Leah saw Ethan's jaw clench.

"Do you know what I think, Ethan?" Jonah asked.

"Because you have been drinking, I do not care what you think," Ethan answered.

Jonah leaned over so that his face was inches

from Ethan's. "I think you are proud. All you Longacres are proud."

Ethan started to rise to his feet. Leah grabbed his arm. "It's only words, Ethan. Ignore him. He's drunk." She knew Ethan rejected violence, but she was angry enough to hit Jonah herself. Why was he spoiling their evening?

Jonah acted as if Leah hadn't even spoken. "You are proud. Your father is proud. Eli would have drunk beer with me."

Ethan shot to his feet. The color had drained from his face, and his hands were balled into fists. "You go too far, Jonah. Do not *ever* say that name to me. You know it is forbidden to speak it."

Jonah reeled backward. He blinked. A low growl tore from his throat, and he stalked off toward the stream.

Ethan took off in the other direction. Leah went after him. She caught up with him far downstream. She wasn't sure anyone had seen what had happened between Ethan and Jonah, but no one had followed them. "Ethan!" she called.

He stopped, then turned slowly. "Leave me be, Leah."

"No," she said, moving closer. "You can't just bring me here and run away. I can figure out that Jonah doesn't like me, maybe because of his sister. I even understand. But I saw your fists. You almost hit him back there. All because he mentioned someone named Eli. What's going on? Who's Eli? You owe me an explanation."

Ethan let out a long, slow, shuddering breath. It took him a long time to answer. At last he said, "Eli is my brother."

FOURTEEN

"Your brother?" Leah wasn't sure she'd heard Ethan correctly. "You mean you have another brother besides Simeon and Nathan?"

Ethan turned away from her. "Yes."

Leah stepped in front of him, refusing to let him walk away. "Tell me about Eli." When he didn't respond, she added, "Please, tell me."

"Eli is older than me. The firstborn." Ethan's words were halting, as if it hurt his throat to speak them.

"How much older?"

"Eight years."

Leah was shocked. "Where is he?"

Ethan shrugged. "I am not sure. I think he still lives here in Indiana."

"You're not *sure*?" she repeated. "When did you last see him?"

"When I was ten."

"You haven't seen your own brother for seven years? But why?" Getting information from Ethan was like pulling teeth. Frustrated, Leah wanted him to tell her everything and get it over with. "You sound ashamed of Eli. Are you?"

"You do not understand, Leah."

"I sure don't," she said, exasperated. "You have a brother no one talks about, or even mentions—I've known you since December and I've never once heard about him—and you won't tell me why. Don't you trust me, Ethan?"

"This has nothing to do with you."

There was no moon, so Leah couldn't see his face, but she could hear the sadness in his voice. She reached out and stroked his arm. "I care about you, Ethan. I don't like to see you hurting. I've always wondered whether you—and even Charity—were keeping something from me."

"How did you know?"

"Little things that were said. Embarrassed silences when something would come up that you both didn't want to talk about. I know now that I wasn't imagining it. Was it Eli? Or is there some other secret?"

"I have no other secrets." He sounded miserable.

"But all the Amish kids know about him, don't they? At least Jonah knows."

"Some know about Eli."

"But not me. Is it because I'm English? An outsider?" Leah's frustration turned into a feeling that she'd been rejected.

"Others know about him only if they are old enough to remember him." Ethan bent so that his forehead was touching Leah's. "We do not speak of him. Rebekah doesn't even know about him."

"Rebekah doesn't know she has another brother?" Leah couldn't believe what Ethan was saying. "Are you joking?"

"She was born after Eli left. And since we never speak of him . . ." Ethan let the sentence trail off.

"But—But—Why not?" Leah sputtered. "What's he done that's so horrible? Is he a criminal or something?"

"You are not Amish, Leah."

"What's that supposed to mean? You've always known I wasn't Amish!"

"It is hard to explain our ways to you."

Leah folded her arms across her chest. "Why don't you try? I promise to act human. Okay?"

Her sarcasm was seemingly lost on Ethan. He gently took her hand and led her to a patch of grassy ground, where he settled her beside him. Leah felt angry and hurt, but she forced herself to keep her temper and to wait in the darkness for him to finally speak.

"Eli was my big brother, and I followed him around like a puppy. He was different from me. Different from all of my family."

"How was he so different?"

"He never loved the land the way Opa, Papa and I do. He didn't like our simple ways. Eli was born smart. He loved books. And learning. When I was six, he was fourteen and in the eighth grade. He went to the English middle school—as we all did. He made straight As."

Leah knew Amish kids left school after the eighth grade because, according to Charity, the Amish saw no need for advanced education. Eventually the Amish teen would take his or her place in the community and therefore had no real need for more schooling. Farming, carpentry work and rearing families were not tasks that needed degrees. Preserving the Amish way of life superseded everything else. "Didn't Eli drop out of school?" she asked.

"No. One of his teachers came out to the farm to talk to Papa. She showed Papa test scores and told him that Eli was very smart—too smart to drop out. She said it would be a sin to let such intelligence go to waste. She talked Papa into letting Eli continue his education."

"That doesn't seem so terrible," Leah said. "Your parents must have been proud of Eli."

"They were."

Instantly Leah realized what Ethan was telling her. Mr. Longacre *had* been proud of Eli. But pride was not a virtue to the Amish. "What happened?"

"Eli was allowed to go to high school. He got on the school bus and rode away each day. He came home and did homework by lamplight. He read books, and more books. As he got older and made friends among the English, he would stay in town with them. It was very hard on Papa because he expected Eli to do his chores and help on the farm. They had harsh words.

Whenever Eli did come home, he brought friends Papa did not like. Finally he stopped coming home.

"It was difficult for me too," Ethan confessed. "I loved them both, and I missed Eli in the family."

Leah could well imagine the scenes. "Is that the reason you didn't run around with your friends when you first turned sixteen? You didn't want to upset your father?"

A low chuckle escaped from Ethan. "You know me well, Leah. Yes. I did not want to disappoint Papa as Eli did."

"You didn't mind quitting school, did you?"

"I am not smart like Eli. Leaving school was not hard for me. Harder for Charity, I think. But not for me."

For Leah, school had never been an option. It was someplace she had to go whether she liked it or not. And for the most part, she liked school. She couldn't imagine not going. "What happened after Eli graduated from high school?"

"It was like chocolate cake and grapefruit juice."

"Fireworks, huh?"

Ethan nodded. "Eli was offered a college scholarship. All paid up."

Leah understood what such an offer meant. "So he had to choose," she stated. "His education or his family."

"I was ten when he left home for good." Ethan's voice grew soft. "Papa wanted Eli to take over the farm. He wanted him to be baptized, and marry, and live as Amish. But Eli said that Amish ways were backward. He said that he did not want to be Amish. He and Papa had very angry words. In the end, Eli left. I still remember the day. Eli and I shared a room. That morning, he packed everything in bags and an old suitcase. He did not have much. I begged him not to go."

Leah heard a catch in Ethan's voice. She felt his pain. "But he went anyway, didn't he?"

"That day Eli said to me, 'Ethan, now you are the oldest son. Papa will not forgive me for this. I am sorry that you are caught in the middle. It will be as if I am dead. No one will speak my name or ever talk about me around here. But I cannot be Amish. I cannot.' "

Leah felt tears swimming in her own eyes as Ethan talked. She could see the scene vividly in her mind's eye. She could feel the immense weight dropped on Ethan's shoulders the day his brother left. "I'm sorry, Ethan."

"That afternoon one of Eli's friends came for him. I stood at the window. I watched him put his things in the car. I watched the car drive away until it was a tiny speck. I've not seen my brother again."

For Leah, many things about Ethan fell into place. Out of respect for his family, Ethan had chosen not to take his fling with the others. Jonah's taunts about Ethan's refusal to run with his friends must have been doubly hard on Ethan. And then Leah had come along. And Ethan had done what nothing else had made him do—he'd dressed English, played English, dated an English girl. He'd done it for her. "Do you know if Eli graduated from college?" she asked.

"I ran into his former teacher once. She told me that she was sorry about what had happened in our family over Eli, but that she had heard that he was getting a degree in education. That he planned to become a teacher—like her. She was proud of that. It made me very sad."

Leah calculated the age difference between Eli and Ethan. "He must be twenty-five by now. If he's a teacher in Indiana, you could find him—"

Ethan sprang to his feet. "I do not want to find him. It is *verboten*—forbidden. I could not betray Papa's wishes."

Leah knew better than to argue. "It was just a thought."

"You think this is foolish, don't you?" Ethan's question floated to her in the dark.

Leah didn't answer right away because she didn't want to upset or hurt him. Nor did she want to seem unsympathetic to the Amish mind-set. Still, it did help her understand Mr. Longacre's coolness toward her. The English way of life had taken one son already.

"Ethan, I really do know what it's like to lose someone you love." Leah chose her words carefully. "I had a grandmother—my father's mother—and for some reason she and my mom never got along with each other. It had something to do with my dad and his leaving us, but I was just a little girl and didn't have a clue.

"Anyway, I loved Grandma Hall with all my heart. She used to sneak into my elementary school during recesses and visit with me on the playground. She brought me cookies and little presents. I still miss her."

"What happened to her?"

"She got sick and died. My mother did let me visit her while she was in the hospital, but it was hard seeing her that way—hooked up to machines and suffering. It scared me." She looked up at Ethan. "Like you, I was also only ten. Grandma died and I went to her funeral. I'll never forget it."

Ethan's arm went around Leah's shoulders. He pulled her close. "This is a sad story, Leah."

"Please listen to what I'm saying. My grandmother's dead, and I'll never see her again on earth. Eli isn't dead. You can see him."

Ethan's arms loosened their hold on her. "It is not that simple. My father would not approve. And so long as I live in my father's house, I must honor and obey him. It is our way."

"Yet it's all right for you to drink and drive cars and sample wordly stuff. You just can't ever speak to your brother again." Leah knew she was testing Ethan's loyalty, but she couldn't help it. Couldn't he see how contradictory, how hypocritical, his ways sounded to her?

Ethan sighed deeply. "I knew you would not understand. I should not have told you."

She took his arm. "I'm glad you told me. Because I want to understand, Ethan. I want to know everything I can about you."

He held her face between the palms of his hands. "And I want to know all about you too, Leah. You are very special to me."

She felt her knees going weak with emotion. She couldn't challenge him again. His brother Eli was a closed subject. Still, Leah couldn't help wondering if her existence too might someday be blotted out by Ethan's family. The notion left her queasy. "Your secret is safe with me, Ethan," she said. But she thought, *Eli does exist. And no amount of pretending will make him disappear.*

She took Ethan's hand. "Come on. Let's go back to the party. Charity might be looking for us."

FIFTEEN

When Leah and Ethan returned to the campsite, the bonfire had died down to a pile of glowing embers. Sleeping bags stretched across blankets and quilts in clusters. Leah heard the soft whispers of conversation mixed with music from radios. She looked around for Charity. "Where do you suppose your sister is?"

"I do not know."

"I don't see Jonah either."

"They are here, I'm sure. Charity would not go off the property."

"I hope you're right. Jonah had too much to drink."

Ethan spread out two sleeping bags. "Come here, Leah. I will tuck you in."

She crawled inside the sleeping bag, and Ethan fastened the side. "I'll bet this is how a caterpillar feels in a cocoon," she said.

Ethan chuckled and wiggled into the sleeping bag next to hers. "Sleep fast. The sun will be up soon."

Leah yawned. She snuggled closer to Ethan. "My nose itches."

He kissed the tip. "Did that help?"

"Much better." She felt Ethan's warm breath against her cheek. Her sleepiness vanished and her heart began to beat faster. "I've never spent the night with a guy before!"

"I am glad I am the first," he whispered. He freed his arms from his sleeping bag and caressed her cheek.

"No fair," she told him. "I can't touch you."

"It is better this way. If you began to touch me, I would not want you to stop."

"Stopping is hard," she said. Her blood sizzled and her pulse pounded.

He nuzzled her neck. "Leah, I would not ever do anything to shame you."

She knew what he meant. He would not pressure her for more. Leah realized how easy it would be to let herself go with him. So very easy. "You are a person of honor," she said. The word sounded old-fashioned, but it was the right word to describe Ethan. He was *honorable.* He didn't know how else to be. He made Leah feel cherished.

"Good night, my Leah." Ethan's arms enveloped her, sleeping bag and all. Soon she heard his rhythmic breathing and knew he'd fallen asleep.

My Leah. She *was* his Leah. For all their differences, for all the chasms that separated them, she belonged to Ethan. And she hadn't an earthly idea what she was going to do about it when the summer ended.

Dawn's pink fingers streaked the sky as Leah struggled to awaken. The aroma of freshly brewing coffee made her stomach growl. Beside her, Ethan's sleeping bag was empty. She sat up and rubbed her sleep-blurred eyes. She saw Ethan hunched down over a small campfire, filling two cups with coffee. She combed her hair with her fingers, wishing she had a brush.

Ethan returned and handed her a coffee cup. "If you'd rather, I will get you a soda."

"No, coffee's fine." Leah took the cup from him and warmed her hands.

They sat together on the quilt and watched the red ball of the sun rise over the dew-drenched meadow. The morning haze began to lift, and the sky turned from pink to blue. The smell of coffee mingled with the scent of sizzling bacon. Leah said, "I had no idea mornings could be so gorgeous. The sun's always up by the time I get to work. I sleep in on the weekends."

"I have always known," Ethan said. "It is my favorite part of the day." His deep love for the land shimmered in his eyes. "Now that you know, maybe you will also want to get up at five-thirty every day."

"Naw," she said, scrunching her face. He laughed.

Charity walked over and sat down with a heavy sigh. She looked haggard. "I thought the morning would never come," she said.

"Where were you all night?" Leah asked.

"I was caring for Jonah. He became very sick." She stole a glance at Ethan, who appeared uninterested.

Leah said, "He drank too much, didn't he?"

Charity nodded. "I'm sure he did not mean to."

Angry at Jonah for spoiling Charity's evening, Leah said, "You should have let him suffer by himself."

"I could not," Charity said miserably. "He had no one else."

"Maybe he'll think twice before drinking that much ever again."

"Maybe."

Ethan spoke. "Jonah is trying to prove he's a man. But this is not the way a man acts."

"Don't criticize him," Charity said testily. "He will find his way back. I know he will."

"It is best if you ride home with Leah and me—"

"We can stop by my apartment and freshen up," Leah interjected. She didn't want Ethan and Charity arguing—especially over Jonah. He wasn't worth it, to her way of thinking.

"I will change my clothes at your place." Charity looked down at the skirt Leah had loaned her. "I'm afraid this is messed up. I will clean it for you."

"It's okay. It'll wash."

"I am sorry, Leah."

Leah didn't care about the skirt. She cared

about Charity, and she hoped her friend wasn't making a mistake in caring about Jonah.

"It's all right," Leah assured Charity. "The important thing is that you're all right. Did you have any fun at all?"

Charity's smile looked wan. "It was not what I expected."

"Maybe next year will be better."

"Maybe." Charity stared out across the meadow. "By next year, perhaps Jonah will have tired of his fling."

Leah hoped so. She recalled the secret of Eli, Ethan and Charity's brother. Would Jonah forsake his Amish upbringing as Eli had? Leah knew Jonah could break Charity's heart.

Leah didn't even let on to Charity that she knew about Eli. But she couldn't look at Rebekah and not think it a shame that the child didn't know she had another brother. As for her feelings toward Mr. Longacre, Leah was torn. Her own father had walked out of her life when she'd been a small child, and all her life she'd wondered why. What had driven him off? She had no answers.

But Mr. Longacre had disowned his eldest son. Eli's desire to go to high school and college seemed such a small deviation from the Amish lifestyle. This sobered Leah and disturbed her greatly. If Mr. Longacre would ignore his own flesh and blood, what chance did *she* have of his ever accepting her, a stranger and English to boot? The problem with the Amish, Leah decided, was that they never made allowances for individuality.

And yet, Leah had to admit that despite its inflexibility, she was attracted to the Amish lifestyle, to the Amish sense of community and togetherness. She wondered why people couldn't have it both ways.

Once the July Fourth weekend was over, the ranks of tourists thinned considerably. Leah went back to work at the inn. Kathy was replaced by an Amish girl named Esther, who was so shy, it was more than a week before Leah heard the girl say a word. No matter how many friendly overtures Leah made, Esther couldn't be coaxed from her shell. If Leah asked her a question, Esther turned bright red, stared down at the floor, and barely mumbled an answer. Leah missed the talkative Kathy immensely.

Leah spent the weekends with Ethan. He arrived at her apartment on Saturday mornings, stayed with friends in town on Saturday nights, and spent all day Sunday with her. This meant that he was not attending Amish church services at all. She couldn't imagine that Ethan's weekend absences won her points with his parents.

She found things to keep her and Ethan busy when they were together. They watched videos, went to movies, skated at The Rink, and drove into the countryside for picnics and shopping sprees. On the first Saturday in August, he took her horseback riding.

"Is he safe?" Leah asked, looking at the big horse standing in the yard of the riding stable. "I don't think he likes me, Ethan."

Ethan shimmied up his mount as if he'd been born to ride a horse. "The owner tells me your horse is very tame. He will not harm you. I thought you once lived in Texas."

The horse turned its neck and stared at Leah as if to say, *"Are you getting on or not?"*

Leah glanced up at Ethan. "You've watched too many movies. Most Texans wisely drive cars." She took a deep breath and put her foot into the stirrup. With an effort, she hauled herself onto the horse's back, then held on to the saddle horn and reins for dear life. "Okay, I'm on."

Ethan laughed aloud. "If you could see your face."

"I'm so glad I'm entertaining you." She shifted. The horse snorted. "How do I put him in gear?"

"Give him some slack on the reins, dig your knees into his side, and he will go."

Leah did as she was told, and the horse broke into a trot. She almost lost her balance, fell forward and hugged the horse's neck. "Where's the brake on this thing?"

Ethan came up alongside and took her horse's bridle, slowing the animal to a walk. "When you want him to stop, pull back on the reins. You must show him who is boss."

"No contest. He's the boss. He's bigger." Leah's legs felt awkward spread around the horse and saddle. "Does this ever get more comfortable?"

"It is customary to feel sore at first. But once you get used to riding—"

"I'll be too old to do it."

They rode a well-defined trail that cut

through the countryside, following a stream. Before long, Leah began to relax.

"I will tell you something," Ethan said, breaking the silence. "I am learning how to drive a car."

"You are? But that's good. Isn't it?" Leah realized he was further defying his father and his Amish upbringing. "Who's teaching you?"

"Jonah."

"I'm sure Jonah gets a thrill out of seeing you try more and more English things."

"You sound as if you do not approve."

"I didn't mean it that way. I think you should learn to drive if you want to. Will you ever own a car?"

"I do not think so."

"Tell me about driving. Do you like it?"

"It is hard not to go too fast. And there is much to remember. A car has many buttons and switches. A horse is much simpler." He patted his horse's neck.

"But a horse doesn't have soft leather seats." Leah squirmed. She couldn't get comfortable in the hard saddle.

"But a car cannot put a soft nose on the back of your neck and nuzzle you."

"I thought that's what guys were for."

Ethan burst out laughing. He looked over at her, his expression growing serious. "Sometimes—more since I have known you—I feel locked up. Like I am inside a box."

She remembered what he'd said about traveling and seeing the world. "I'd feel bad if you were trying things just because of me."

"It is my right to test, remember?"

"Well, if you ever want to get away from all this, come see me. Neil owns a farm, you know, so it won't be a total change."

"What kind of farm?" Ethan sounded interested.

"Oh, not like your farm," Leah added hastily. "Neil bought this big piece of land at an auction. He has a big house on it. You see, he lived in Detroit all his life and decided to retire out in the wide-open spaces."

"A farm that does not grow food?" Ethan sounded amazed. "Does he have a barn for dairy cows?"

"He keeps cars in the barn."

Ethan turned and stared, as if to see if she was teasing him. "Cars? In a barn?"

"He collects antique cars." Leah felt almost apologetic. "They're worth a lot of money. And the barn's specially made to keep the cars well preserved."

"Land is the greatest thing a man can own, but I cannot imagine owning a farm that grows nothing, has no livestock, and stores cars in a good barn." Ethan shook his head.

Leah should have figured that to Ethan's frugal Amish mind, owning land merely for the pleasure of having space around you would make no sense. Worse, it made her lifestyle seem wasteful and foolish. "Collecting cars is Neil's hobby. Sort of like that train we saw at the toy store. Just bigger. Don't you Amish have any hobbies?"

"Working a farm does not leave us with much extra time, Leah. Many of us would like to be farmers, but farmland is not plentiful any longer, so we must become carpenters or have our own stores. And I do not want you thinking that I am critical of Neil. It is just that to hear of good land lying fallow is a shock to me."

"I guess I understand," Leah told him. "I've just never thought of it that way before. Mom and I have lived in apartments and trailers all our lives, so being out in the country, with all this land around me, is a real change. I didn't even like it at first. It was lonely and miles from anything that even resembled a mall."

"Do you still not like living there?"

"I'm used to it now. And being here all summer—going out to your farm and seeing how much you like the great outdoors—has made me feel better about it."

Ethan stared off into the distance, across open fields and rolling meadows. "I cannot imagine being stuck someplace where there is no land around me. Where there are only cars and noise and too many people. The land makes me feel connected to God and all that he has made."

Leah couldn't imagine not being around cars and people and some kind of city life. She had not felt the gap between herself and Ethan so keenly in weeks. She felt it now, just as she felt the discomfort of the hard saddle and the plodding horse beneath her. Their ways of life were poles apart. Could anything ever close the gap between them?

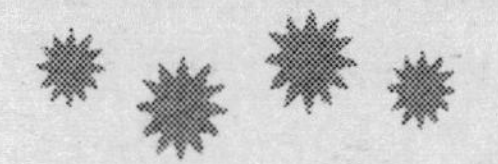

Sixteen

"Hi, honey. How are you doing?"

"Mom? Where are you?" Leah hugged the phone receiver to her ear.

"Hawaii," her mother said.

"You sound like you're next door."

Her mother took a breath. "Neil and I are spending more time here before we head back to the mainland. It's been a fabulous trip. Did you get my postcards?"

Leah glanced at the colorful pictures lining her refrigerator door. "Sure did. It sounds like you've been having a good time."

"Oh, have we ever! I'm sorry you missed it, Leah. How's your summer been?"

"I'm having a great time too."

"Really? I was hoping you weren't having regrets about not coming along."

"No regrets," Leah told her.

"That's good." Her mother sounded relieved. "Well, Neil's taken a hundred pictures and made a ton of tapes with the camcorder. I can't wait for you to see them."

"When will you be home?"

"In two weeks. Summer's almost over, you know. School will be starting soon."

Leah's heart lurched. Her gaze flew quickly to the calendar on her kitchen wall, and she saw that August was well under way. She'd been so caught up in her everyday life, she'd forgotten how close it was to the start of the new school year. And to going home. Somehow, it had seemed as if her life in Nappanee would go on forever. "I guess you're right."

"When do you see Dr. Thomas again?"

"Not until fall, I think. I have an appointment card around here somewhere."

"How have you been feeling?"

"I feel fine." Leah hated being reminded that her health wasn't perfect. There were days now when she never even thought about it. And then there were days when she thought about it a lot. The soreness in her knee came and went. When it came, she took pain relievers and tried not to bend too much.

"We've got back-to-school shopping to do," her mother said. "Why don't I come and help you pack up your things on the twenty-third?"

"Um—I guess that's all right. I have to tell Mrs. Stoltz exactly when I'll be leaving."

"What would you think about driving into Chicago to shop after you come home? I've heard the bargains there are fantastic."

"Sure, Mom. That'll be fine."

"Then it's settled. I'll call you when we get back to our place," her mother added cheerfully. "See you soon. And Neil says hi."

After hanging up, Leah stood holding the receiver and listening to the dial tone. Her wonderful summer was almost over, her time with Ethan almost gone. She finally hung up the phone and leaned her forehead against the wall. She couldn't imagine her days without him. "Oh, Ethan," she sighed. "What are we going to do?"

Mrs. Stoltz needed some fresh produce, so Leah drove out to the Amish stand. She looked for Rebekah among the Amish kids working, but she couldn't find her. A girl's voice said, "If you're looking for Rebekah, she left early today."

Leah turned to face Martha Dewberry. Martha was dressed in a short summer Amish dress of pale green and was holding a basket of beets. Leah said, "Oh . . . well, thanks."

"Could I help you?"

"I—um—just need some vegetables for the inn."

"I'll show you what is freshest today. I know how Mrs. Stoltz likes high quality."

Leah reminded herself that in such a small town, everybody knew everybody else. It was no surprise that Martha could pick just the right things for Mrs. Stoltz. Still, Leah disliked tagging along behind Martha while Martha chose items from the stacks of vegetables and fruits.

"There," Martha finally said, handing Leah two sacks full of food. "This should be enough."

Leah paid at the cashier and carried the sacks to her car. Martha opened the car door for her. "I guess you'll be going home soon," she said. "You're still in school, aren't you?"

"Yes, I'm leaving soon. Yes, I still have another year before I graduate."

Martha smiled, reminding Leah of a contented cat. "Then your summer here has been successful?"

"I've had a good time, if that's what you mean." Tension crept up Leah's neck. "I like it here and I've made some good friends."

"Will you come back?"

Leah squared her chin. "I might. If I'm invited."

"It is not easy being Amish for you English. One summer is not a true test of being one of us, you know."

Is that what Martha thinks? That I'm trying to be one of them? "I guess it's never good to try and be something you're not," Leah said. "But I think it's okay to sample different things in life. Isn't that what you Amish do when you take a fling?"

Martha's cheeks colored, and Leah knew that her barb had hit home. "You are right. Experimentation is not a bad thing," Martha said. "Making the *wrong* choice is the bad thing."

Tired of dancing around the subject, Leah blurted out, "Is that what you think Ethan's done? Made a bad choice by being with me all summer?"

Martha shrugged. "It is not for me to say.

Ethan is a grown man. But the summer is almost over. And you will be leaving because you are English and have another life away from here. But I will remain, because this is my place. And Ethan will be here too, because this is his place. I offer you no bad feelings, Leah. It is the way things are."

Leah turned away. Anger bubbled inside her. But she could not dispute anything that Martha had said. She had heard that patience was a virtue, and in this case, it was. Martha had patiently waited on the sidelines all summer, knowing full well that autumn would come, and with it, Leah's departure.

Partly because Martha had made her angry, partly because she just wanted to see her friends, Leah drove up to the farmhouse. She struggled to calm herself. She didn't want any of them to know she was upset. There was nothing anyone could do. As Martha had said, "It is the way things are."

Leah parked her car, opened the door and felt a wet, stinging smack against her leg. Startled, she looked down to see water soaking the leg of her jeans. She looked up to see Simeon gaping at her from the corner of the house, a water balloon poised in one hand. "Leah," he called. "I'm sorry. I was trying to hit Rebekah."

Rebekah darted from behind Leah and the old wagon wheel by the flowers, a water balloon balanced in each hand. Her sleeves were rolled up, she was barefoot, and the front of her pale yellow dress was soaked. "Oh, Leah. Are you all right?" the little girl asked, wide-eyed.

"I'm fine. I was planning on taking a shower later anyway, and now you've saved me the trouble. What's going on?"

"We're having a water fight," Rebekah said with a toothy grin.

"Does your mother know?"

"Oh yes. It is fun."

Leah took one of the balloons from Rebekah and juggled it lightly in one hand. "Fun, you say?" Without warning, she spun, heaved the balloon and hit Simeon squarely in the chest. She grabbed Rebekah and yelled, "Run!"

The two of them dashed like rabbits toward the barn, Rebekah shrieking and Leah laughing. Simeon followed in hot pursuit. At the barn, Leah rounded the corner and crouched. "Where're more balloons?" she asked breathlessly.

Giggling, Rebekah handed her the one she still carried. "This is all I have."

"You don't have more? Uh-oh. I think we're in big trouble."

"Follow me," Rebekah said. "We'll hide."

They crawled on all fours inside the barn. At the far end, Leah saw Ethan, busy heaving forkfuls of hay into stalls. He didn't see them. "Shhh," Leah said. "He might tell Simeon where we are." They scurried into an empty stall and peeked through the slats.

Simeon raced into the barn, his water balloon held high. He skidded to a stop. "Where are they?"

"Who?" Ethan asked, looking up.

"Leah and Rebekah. They're in here."

"I do not think so."

"Help me look."

Leah watched as Simeon and Ethan made their way slowly toward them. Rebekah's eyes danced and she clapped her hand over her mouth. Leah clutched the balloon and held her breath. Just as the two brothers passed their hiding place, she sprang to her feet and tossed the balloon. But Simeon, seeing it coming, dropped and rolled out of harm's way. The balloon landed with a splat on the side of Ethan's face.

"Oops," Leah said as Ethan whipped around. "Sorry about that." She offered an innocent smile and a shrug.

Simeon held his fire, and Rebekah looked up expectantly at Ethan. Ethan looked so comical standing in front of her dripping wet that Leah started laughing.

"Do you think this is funny?" Ethan asked with mischief in his eyes.

"Hysterical," Leah managed between laughs.

"I have one balloon left," Simeon said, offering his prize to his brother.

"One balloon is not enough." Lightning fast, Ethan caught Leah's arms.

She squealed as he heaved her over his shoulder like a sack of grain. "Put me down!"

"I will," Ethan said, striding purposefully out of the barn.

"Hold your breath!" Rebekah yelled. "You're in for a dunking!"

From her upside-down vantage point, all Leah saw was the ground. Then Ethan stopped, and the view of the ground gave way to one of the animal-watering trough. "Don't you dare, Ethan Longacre!" she wailed. But to no avail. Leah screeched as Ethan plopped her into the water. She came up sputtering and splashing.

She grabbed at Ethan's shirtfront as Rebekah shoved him from behind. He lost his balance and fell smack on top of Leah. They both yelped and floundered, sending water every which way.

Rebekah and Simeon came over to see and also landed in the wooden trough. All four of them sloshed around like floppy fish. Struggling to get out, Leah slipped and went down in the mud. Ethan came over the side next and slid beside her, stomach first. Leah burst out laughing again. Ethan flipped a wad of mud at her. She retaliated, and soon they were tossing handfuls of mud at each other.

By the time Leah finally wiggled away, she was coated with gooey mud and Martha's words were all but forgotten. "I should murder you."

"We Amish are nonviolent, remember?"

Leah was laughing and shaking mud off her hands and arms. "I'm a mess. Mrs. Stoltz will never send me out to buy vegetables again."

"You're a pretty mess," Ethan said, dipping into the water and wiping her cheek.

Rebekah leaped out of the trough. "Come, Leah. Let's go clean up. We'll use the pump by the house."

Ethan helped Leah to her feet. "Should I?"

she asked. "I don't want to get you all in trouble with your parents."

"Charity and Mama have gone into town, and Papa is working with Opa in a field far away from the house. Come and clean up," Ethan urged her.

At the house, Rebekah told Elizabeth and Oma about the water fight, while Leah finished washing up at the kitchen sink what she hadn't cleaned off at the outside pump.

"Do you want to change into clean clothes?" Oma asked Leah.

"This is fine. Really," she added when the older woman looked skeptical. Leah didn't want to be a bother. "I can stop by my apartment on my way back to the inn. I've been away too long as it is. Mrs. Stoltz is expecting me to bring fresh vegetables in time for supper. Thanks anyway."

"As you wish," Oma said. Her face was thin, worn by years of hard work. Her eyes were the palest blue. She looked at Leah with kindness. "My grandchildren like you very much, Leah. And I have always found them to be very good judges of character."

Surprised by Oma's words, Leah offered a shy smile. "That's nice of you to say."

"You are welcome, Leah," Oma answered.

With sunlight streaming through the kitchen window and bathing her face in gentle light, Oma didn't seem stern or formidable to Leah. In some ways, she looked like Leah's grandmother, caring and compassionate. Leah felt a lump of longing in her throat. "I have to go," she said.

Leah hurried outside and down the porch steps. Rebekah and Ethan were waiting for her by her car.

Rebekah took Leah's hand. "You're fun, Leah."

"You're fun too."

"I love you," Rebekah added, hugging Leah.

Leah's eyes filled with moisture. "I love you back," she told the child.

In another two weeks, Leah's mother would be coming, and Leah would be leaving Nappanee, possibly for good. With time closing in on her, she decided that she wanted to see Charity and Rebekah more often. The following Friday after work, she screwed up her courage and drove back out to the farm—this time, to stay for a long visit. She didn't care how much Mr. Longacre scowled at her. She wasn't going to be intimidated.

Leah drove down the road talking to herself and building up her courage. In the distance, flashes of blue light caught her eye. She squinted. In the shimmering heat from the asphalt, a mass of cars and people took shape. Red lights flickered among the blue. The activity seemed to be close to the produce stand. Leah's heart leaped into her throat. She pushed down on the accelerator. The car sped forward. Leah saw police cars everywhere. And ambulances. And emergency medical technicians in uniforms. Something had happened. Something terrible.

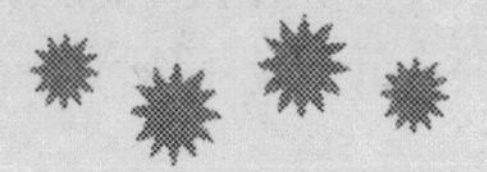

SEVENTEEN

Leah had to park on the shoulder of the road, yards away from the roadside disaster, because of the crowd. She leaped from the car and started running, stopping only when a police officer forced her to. "Can't go closer, miss," he warned.

"But they're my friends." She strained to see around him and the knot of people. Half the produce stand was fractured. Splintered wood and smashed vegetables and fruit lay scattered on the ground. The scene was one of total devastation. Leah felt sick. "What happened?"

"You'll have to step back, miss," the officer said firmly, not bothering to answer her question. "We've got injured people here."

"Please, let me through," Leah pleaded.

The officer turned to continue directing people away.

Frantically, Leah grabbed a bystander. "Do you know what happened?"

A plump, middle-aged man wore a grim expression. "Some guy lost control of his pickup truck, swerved and plowed into the stand. My wife and I were standing on the other side or we would have been wiped out too."

"Did it just happen?"

"Maybe twenty minutes ago. They think he was drinking, or maybe had a heart attack at the wheel. He never slowed down, just smashed into them."

Leah craned her neck and saw a blue truck with an out-of-state license plate, nosedown in a ditch in the field behind the stand. The split-rail fence had been snapped like toothpicks, and rows of corn had been flattened. With a start, Leah realized that the truck was on Longacre property. She pushed her way through the onlookers and edged around to the back of the area. A group of Amish kids, many sobbing and holding on to one another, were huddled on makeshift seats of cardboard cartons and plastic baskets. Some were holding towels to their faces, arms and legs. Police officers and rescue workers were trying their best to comfort them.

Anxiously Leah scanned the group for familiar faces. *Rebekah. Where's Rebekah?* Leah tried to get closer, but another officer stopped her. "Sorry, miss. You'll have to stand back."

"I know these people. They're my friends."

"We have injuries. I can't let you in there."

"Who got hurt?" Leah asked. The officer wasn't listening. He had turned to talk to a rescue worker.

Frantic and frustrated, Leah looked around and down. For the first time, she noticed smears of blood on the ground. Shoving past the police officer, she ran toward the Amish kids. She was on her knees in front of one of Rebekah's friends, Karen. "Tell me who's hurt." Leah took Karen's hands. "Please. Where's Rebekah Longacre?"

Karen looked at Leah, a mix of shock and horror on her face. "The ambulance took her."

Leah felt queasy. "Was she . . . is she okay?"

Karen shrugged just as Leah felt the police officer's beefy hand on her shoulder. "I told you to stay back," the man barked.

Shakily Leah stood, fighting the urge to scream. "Where did the ambulance go?"

The officer said, "Nappanee Hospital emergency room."

Leah ran back to her car. Her hands were shaking so badly she could hardly get the key into the ignition. When she did get the engine started, she gunned it and made a U-turn in the middle of the blocked highway, heading back toward town. All the way there, she prayed, "Dear God, please let Rebekah be okay. Please!"

Leah raced into the emergency room. In one corner she saw the entire Longacre family—from little Nathan to the grandparents. In their quaint Amish clothing, surrounded by the high-tech decor of the hospital lobby, they struck a discordant note. Seeing Leah, Ethan came quickly to face her.

Leah grabbed his shirt. "How is she?"

"We do not know yet," Ethan said grimly. "We only just got here ourselves, and the doctors haven't told us anything."

"I was on my way to your place when I saw

. . . I saw—" Leah's sobs choked off her words.

"We were working in the fields when we heard the bell. Mama rang it and we came running."

Leah remembered the big bell that hung on the front porch. It was rung for meals and for emergencies. When it sounded in the middle of the day, all the Amish came quickly to see what was wrong. "Oh, Ethan, this is so horrible! Why did it have to happen?"

"Come," he said. "Sit with us."

She followed him to where his father and grandfather stood, their eyes closed, heads bowed. The family had formed a tight circle with chairs, and Tillie Longacre sat ramrod straight, clutching Oma's hand. Charity, Simeon, and Elizabeth were slumped, their cheeks streaked with tears. Sarah, looking very pregnant, held baby Nathan. Her husband paced the floor.

Leah felt like an intruder, but she couldn't be shut out now. She wouldn't allow it. She crouched in front of Ethan's mother. "I'm sorry, Mrs. Longacre," Leah whispered. "Really, really sorry."

"My child is in God's hands now. He will care for her."

Ethan took Leah to one side, and soon Charity joined them. Leah told Charity what she'd heard at the scene of the accident, then asked, "Do you know anything else?"

"Rebekah had her back turned and didn't see the truck coming. She never had time to jump out of the way." Charity's voice cracked.

"You mean the truck ran over her?" Leah thought she was going to be ill.

"We are not sure, but that's the way it looks."

"Then she could be . . . she could be—"

"Do not say the words," Charity interrupted. "Do not even think them."

Leah turned back toward Ethan. "Rebekah's got to be all right. She has to be."

"The produce stand was well made," Charity offered. "It was strong and sturdy. Perhaps it shielded Rebekah somehow."

"Wood is no match for metal," Ethan said bitterly.

All afternoon, the lobby filled with Amish as word spread about Rebekah. Through the sliding glass doors, Leah saw a parking lot full of dark buggies and horses. The men came to Jacob, the women to Tillie. Leah heard one man say, "We are all giving blood, Jacob. Your little one may have need of it."

Leah watched as they rolled up their sleeves and followed nurses down the hall to the lab. She stood. "Maybe I can give blood too," she told Ethan, starting down the hall.

He followed her quickly. "You do not have to do this. There will be enough who give."

"Don't you want my blood? Is it too English?" His face colored, and she regretted her words. "Forgive me, Ethan. I didn't mean it. I just want to do something for Rebekah."

"There is nothing to forgive, Leah. I know how you care about my sister."

At the lab, Leah collected paperwork from a technician and began filling it out. When she got to the box requesting information about diseases or illnesses she may have had, she stopped writing. *Cancer.* The word jumped off the page at her. Her blood ran cold. She took it over to the tech. "Excuse me, but what if I've had one of these problems?"

"Then you can't donate blood."

"But why? I'm sure the problem's gone."

"Sorry. That's the rule. We can't take a

chance of passing on serious medical conditions to others." He reached for the paper.

Leah wadded it up, tossed it on the desk and fled the area.

Ethan caught up with her in the hallway. "Stop, Leah."

Crying, she struggled to get away.

"It is not your fault that you had cancer," Ethan said. "Rebekah has plenty of blood donors. Do not concern yourself."

"It's not fair. It isn't, Ethan! There's nothing I can do for her. Nothing."

He held her while she cried. Finally he fumbled for his big handkerchief and wiped her cheeks. "Come. I must get back to the lobby in case the doctor comes to tell us something."

Leah went with him to the lobby, where a doctor in a white lab coat was standing with the family. Flecks of dried blood splattered his shoe coverings. He looked grim, and Leah felt her mouth go cotton dry. He was saying, "We've finally gotten your daughter stabilized and moved up to intensive care."

"How is she?" Jacob Longacre asked, his voice thick with emotion.

"In all honesty, sir, she's in critical condition,

with massive internal injuries. Right now, she's comatose and on a respirator."

"But she is alive," Tillie Longacre said.

The doctor nodded.

"May we see her?" Mr. Longacre asked.

"Yes. ICU is on the third floor. The nurses up there will take you to her." The doctor put a hand on Mrs. Longacre's shoulder. "We're doing everything medically possible for her."

Leah realized that the doctor didn't sound hopeful at all. Mrs. Longacre held her head high. Her eyes were diamond bright with tears. "We will go to her." Calmly, she walked arm in arm with her husband to the elevator, and the rest of the family followed like ducklings. Leah fell into step beside Ethan, hardly daring to take a breath, terrified that she might use up all the oxygen in the room and not leave enough for anybody else.

In the ICU area, a nurse took the group into a glass-walled cubicle where Rebekah lay on a bed, hooked to wires and machines. Green blips trailed across the faces of monitors. Electronic beeps punctuated the silence. And the ominous hiss of the respirator spoke of the fragility of Rebekah's life. Leah stared mutely. Rebekah looked like a fractured china doll. Her face was bruised and her arms were in splints. The tube from the respirator protruded from her mouth, held in place by crisscrosses of papery white tape. An IV bag hung from a pole, a long tube running down to the needle inserted under the skin of her hand. Her tiny body hardly made a mound beneath the sheets.

Seeing Rebekah lying so still and unmoving was more than Leah could bear. Feeling lightheaded, she held on to the wall with one hand and moved down the hallway, hoping she wouldn't pass out. Just when she thought she wasn't going to make it, she felt Ethan's strong arm around her waist. "Are you all right?" he asked.

She shook her head, not trusting her voice.

"Sit." He led her to a waiting area and settled her into a chair. "Take deep breaths," he told her.

Leah gulped air and then, finding her voice, managed to say, "Go on back and be with your family."

"I don't want to leave you."

"Please, go on. Your place is with them."

Ethan rose. "I'll be back soon."

Leah watched him hurry away. She hugged her arms and rocked back and forth in the chair. Outside the window of the waiting area, sunlight beat down. She could feel the heat through the glass. Outside, it was summer and the air was hot. But inside, Leah was cold. Very, very cold.

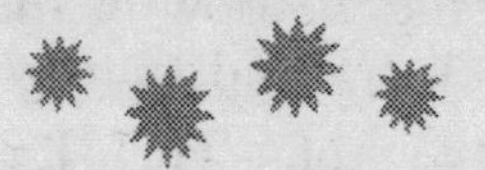

EIGHTEEN

Throughout the long night, Rebekah clung to life. The family was allowed to visit her in ten-minute intervals twice an hour, so everyone took shifts, going in two by two. One of the nurses explained that although Rebekah was in a coma, she might be able to hear, so she suggested that they say positive, encouraging things. "Let her know you love her," the nurse told them.

Leah staked out a place on one of the utilitarian sofas in the waiting area. She didn't care whether the entire Longacre family wanted her around or not. She wasn't going to leave with Rebekah's life hanging in the balance.

Whenever it was Ethan's turn to see his little

sister, Leah went with him. She slipped her hand into Rebekah's and squeezed gently. The child's skin felt cool. "Hi," Leah whispered, close to Rebekah's ear. "It's Leah, your old hospital roommate. Can you hear me? Please wake up, Rebekah."

Only the hiss of the respirator answered Leah.

"You've got to wake up, Rebekah." Leah bit her lip, trying to keep her voice low and calm. "Who's going to take care of your chickens? You're the only one who knows how to really and truly take care of them."

The green line showing Rebekah's heartbeat marched unchanging across the monitor.

"You know I can't tell one chicken from another. How will I know which one is mine if you don't tell me?" Leah asked.

Leah felt Ethan's hand on her shoulder. He crouched beside her, enveloping Leah's hand in his. He whispered something in German in Rebekah's ear. "Come back to us, little one," he added in English. "Do you not know how we love you? Can you not see how we want you to smile at us?"

His quiet voice and simple pleas practically unraveled Leah. "I'll take you for a ride in my car," she promised the child on the bed. "Wouldn't you like that? You can ride up front and wave at all your friends."

"Little sister," Ethan said. "I will let you hold the buggy reins. I am sorry I have always told you no before. But now they will be yours. I will ride beside you and you can make old Bud step high."

Their ten minutes were up. Rebekah had neither moved nor responded. Shakily Leah left with Ethan and returned to the waiting room. Leah slumped into a chair and buried her face in her hands. "When we were in the hospital together last December, it was different," she told Ethan. "Rebekah was sick, but she could talk and smile. Now she's completely helpless. I'm afraid."

"Many people are praying for her," Ethan said. "There is a constant prayer vigil, day and night."

The news comforted Leah. And it gave her hope. Surely, if so many prayers were being said on Rebekah's behalf, how could a loving God turn a deaf ear to them?

Throughout the next day, Amish friends and neighbors came to check on Rebekah and comfort her family. Women brought food-filled baskets so that the Longacres would not have to buy food in the hospital cafeteria. Church elders came, somber men in dark suits, holding their hats in their hands, offering quiet prayers with Jacob and his sons. Leah watched it all, like a parade that she didn't belong to and couldn't get in step with. She knew she stuck out in her English clothes. But she couldn't leave. And she felt that Ethan wanted her with him. They talked little but simply sat in the corner together, their arms and shoulders touching. It comforted Leah to be near him. She hoped her presence offered him some measure of comfort too.

Jonah arrived around noon. He was dressed Amish, and Leah realized it was the only time she'd seen him dressed that way. He looked big and rawboned, ill at ease in the confines of the hospital. Charity went to him, and they stared mutely into each other's eyes. Jonah did not go in to see Rebekah, but when Charity returned from a visit, he sat with her, shielding her protectively with his large body.

Several doctors came to check on Rebekah:

an orthopedist, a neurologist, a critical care physician, and an internist. Each doctor told the family the same thing. "No change. The next forty-eight hours will be her most critical."

That evening, Jacob sent his exhausted parents home. "Your collapse will not bring Rebekah back to us," he told Opa. And to Sarah, he said, "Go get some rest, daughter. You must think now of your own child." Baby Nathan had been taken away earlier by friends who would care for him until the family returned home.

In the early hours of the morning, unable to sleep on the lumpy sofa, Leah ventured down the quiet halls to the elevator. On the ground floor, she found a small chapel, dimly lit and as quiet as a tomb. Sighing, she slid into one of the short rows of pews and bowed her head. Her mind went blank. She wasn't sure what to say to God anymore. She'd already made a hundred promises to him if he'd only make Rebekah well. Now, in this place dedicated to prayer, Leah felt empty and desolate.

She thought about her stay in the hospital and her terror when she'd been told by the doctors that they wanted to amputate her leg. And she remembered how Rebekah and Charity and

Ethan had come into her life and made her less fearful. Now she felt helpless and useless.

"Leah." Ethan's voice interrupted her thoughts. "How are you?" He slipped into the pew.

"Not too good," she answered truthfully. "I'm really scared, Ethan. I'm scared that Rebekah isn't ever going to wake up."

"She hasn't once acted as if she's really here with us," he admitted. "But I will not give up hope."

"I keep thinking about Gabriella and how she kept showing up last December. Where is she now when we need her? She's an angel! So why doesn't she *do* something?"

"What if she wasn't really an angel?" he asked. "What if there is some other explanation?"

Leah shook her head. "I was so sure she was. And you told me that you thought so too."

"All we know for certain is that we cannot explain her strange comings and goings. But even if she is an angel, you cannot expect her to show up in every crisis."

"I'm not asking that she show up in every crisis. But Rebekah needs her now. She should be here. What kind of a guardian angel is she anyway? Why wasn't she on duty when that truck went out of control?"

"Angels are not servants of people. They are servants of God."

"Then God should have sent Gabriella to stop the accident from happening in the first place."

Ethan took a deep breath and smoothed Leah's hair. "But God did not. I do not understand why either. But he did not stop the accident."

Leah laid her head against Ethan's broad chest and began to cry softly.

On Sunday, while the Amish community attended church and prayed for Rebekah and her family, the Longacres remained in the ICU waiting room. Leah stayed also, knowing she couldn't return to her apartment as long as Rebekah was in a coma. The medical tests on Rebekah continued to be discouraging, but still Leah clung to hope. That evening, she called Mrs. Stoltz and quit her job.

"How is the little girl?" Mrs. Stoltz asked.

"No change," Leah said sadly.

On Monday morning the doctors arrived, their expressions unreadable, making Leah feel especially uneasy. She had once seen such carefully guarded looks on the faces of her own doctors before they'd delivered the devastating news that she had bone cancer.

The neurologist held a clipboard and spoke directly to Jacob and Tillie. "We've repeated tests on Rebekah for days now," he said in a kind but firm voice. "I'm sorry to have to tell you this, but Rebekah has no higher brain activity. She hasn't had much since she was brought in, but still we wanted to give her every opportunity for recovery. Medically, your daughter is brain dead, Mr. Longacre. The only thing keeping her alive is the machines. I want your permission to turn the machines off and let her body join her spirit."

In the stunned silence, no one spoke. Leah wanted to scream at him. She wanted to strike him. She wanted to knock him down and step on him. She stood frozen to the floor and watched Tillie's face crumble with grief and a trail of tears run down Jacob's craggy cheeks. "You are sure of this?"

The doctor held out a long piece of paper with computer-drawn squiggles on it. "This is her EEG, a measurement of her brain activity from the time she was brought in. As you can see, the line gets progressively flatter. And her reflexes are gone. Plus, her pupils are fixed and dilated. All these factors convince me of the diagnosis."

Jacob stared long and hard into the doctor's face. Tillie hung on his arm, as if it were her sole means of support. "We will tell her goodbye," Jacob finally said.

Leah trembled. Why didn't he fight? Why didn't he yell no? How could he accept the doctor's word so completely? Doctors could be wrong. Tests could be incorrect. Hadn't that been true in Leah's own case?

The doctor said, "Take all the time you need." As Jacob turned to lead his family toward their final visit into the ICU cubicle, the doctor added, "Even if Rebekah had awakened, sir, she would never have been normal. There was simply too much damage."

Jacob nodded, then stepped inside the cubicle.

Leah trailed behind hesitantly, acutely aware that she was not family but only a bystander in Rebekah's life. So she stood outside the enclosure, her palms pressed against the glass, watching. One by one, each member of Rebekah's family bent and kissed the little girl's cheek. They surrounded the bed, hovering like darkly dressed angels, holding hands and bowing their heads. Leah could hear them murmuring in German, and she could see the expressions of quiet acceptance on their faces.

Leah felt numb all over, as if all the blood had been drained from her body and replaced with ice water. She couldn't accept this. It was horrible and undeserved sentence on a sweet, loving child with her whole life ahead of her. Perhaps the Longacres could see it as God's will, but Leah could not. God was unfair!

When the family finished praying, they sang a hymn in German, then touched Rebekah one last time and left. Leah rode down with them in the elevator. In the parking lot, she blinked in the bright sun. She had not been outside in days. She heard Opa say, "The buggy is over here, Jacob."

As they started toward it, Leah took Ethan's hand, holding him back. "Ethan, please, don't go yet. Tell me what to do. I don't know what to do now."

He stroked her cheek. "Now we go home and prepare for Rebekah's wake and funeral."

"May I come?" she asked in a small voice.

"Certainly, you may come. For now, go home, get some rest. Come to the house tomorrow morning."

"I—I'm not one of you—"

Ethan silenced her by placing the tips of his fingers against her lips. "Rebekah would want you with us," he said. "Charity and I will help you. You will not be alone."

"Should I tell anyone? I—I was thinking of your brother, Eli."

She felt Ethan stiffen. "There is no way to tell him."

"I guess it wouldn't make sense, would it? I mean, he never knew of Rebekah in life. Why should he know of her now that she's—" Leah stopped, unable to say the last word.

The buggy pulled to a stop beside them, and Ethan climbed aboard. His father handed him the reins. Leah heard Ethan say, *"Ya,"* and watched him slap the reins on the horse's rounded rump. She stood in the parking lot, in the hot August-sunshine, and listened to the clop of the animal's hooves on the asphalt. Ethan guided the plain black buggy into the flow of auto traffic. Leah watched it wind its way slowly up the road toward the outskirts of town.

Numb, Leah went to her car. The surface looked dull. She could barely see her reflection in the chrome and mirrors, and what she could see looked distorted. Just as she felt on the inside—deformed and misshapen. Rebekah Longacre was gone. For her there would be no miracle, no restoration of her life to those who loved her. The heavens were silent. God had turned a deaf ear to the prayers and pleas of Amish and English alike. Rebekah was dead. Dead.

NINETEEN

Leah slept fitfully, waking with sudden starts, and, remembering that Rebekah was dead, cried herself back to sleep. Early in the morning, she gave up on sleep, dressed in dark, somber clothes, and drove out to the farm.

When she arrived, the yard was already full of black carriages. Realizing that her red convertible stuck out like a sore thumb, Leah left it at the very edge of the property, on the far end from where the accident had happened. At the site of the accident, Leah saw that every scrap of wood had been cleaned up. All that remained as witness to the horrible event were the smashed rows of corn.

Leah walked toward the farmhouse. Even so

early in the morning, the air seemed stagnant. The heat rose off the ground in waves, making her hair stick to the back of her neck. She found Charity in the front yard, sitting beside the wagon wheel, hugging her knees, her eyes red and puffy. Leah sat down beside her. "Hi. I couldn't stay away any longer."

"I miss Rebekah, Leah. All night, I kept waking up and looking over to her side of the bed. It was empty. Only Rose sat up on the pillow. Like she was waiting for Rebekah to come to bed. I could not bear to even look at her doll."

Fresh tears pooled in Leah's eyes as Charity talked. "I didn't sleep much either." Leah sniffed hard. "Will you tell me what's going to happen? I—I've never been to an Amish funeral."

"The ones I've been to have been for old people. They are expected to die." Charity dabbed at her eyes with a white handkerchief. "But I will tell you what to expect." She sat up straighter. "The Amish undertaker has taken Rebekah's body from the hospital. Papa and Ethan and Opa worked most of the night to build her coffin in the barn. Usually, coffins are made by others, but Papa wanted to make Rebekah's with his own hands."

Leah stared off toward the barn, imagining the sad sound of hammers banging long into the night.

Charity continued. "Other men picked up the coffin this morning and took it to the undertaker's. The hearse will return with it this afternoon for the viewing."

Suddenly it struck Leah that everyone in the community would be arriving to see Rebekah's body lying in the coffin. She shuddered, not certain she could participate in the ritual.

"Many people are helping us now," Charity said. "The men are doing the chores. The women are cleaning the house and setting up for the funeral tomorrow morning. Tomorrow we will have a church service here. Then we will all go to the graveyard at the back of our farm for the burial. Afterward, people will come back here for a meal and help us clear the house of the extra chairs and things. Then everybody will go home."

And life will go on, Leah thought. Chores would be done, cows milked, chickens fed, gardens tilled. Rebekah would be under the ground, and life would go on. She turned to Charity. "You're burying her on the farm?"

"Our family has lived here for many years. In time, all of us will be buried on this land. It is ours."

Leah recalled movies in which cemeteries were portrayed as dark, creepy places where the dead haunted the living. But here, in this land of the Amish, cemeteries were merely resting places for loved ones. There was nothing ghoulish about cemeteries. "What should I do?"

"Just be with us."

Leah plucked a flower from the flower bed and rolled it between her fingers. "Can I send flowers for her funeral?"

Charity shook her head. "That is not done. Amish bury plainly, just as we live."

"Where's Ethan?" All at once, Leah ached to see him, to touch him.

"He is at the family cemetery. He is digging our sister's grave."

Leah followed Charity's directions to the family cemetery, located beyond the barn and the woods, at the back side of the property. She passed the garden and remembered the first day she'd come to the farm and how Rebekah had run to meet her. Leah turned her head. She passed the chicken coop and the barn, remembered the day of the water fight, and felt a lump the size of a fist clog her throat.

Leah skirted the woods and saw a short white picket fence marking off an enclosure of well-kept grass. Within, she saw headstones. She entered by a small gate, covered with an arched arbor, heavy with jasmine and morning-glory vines. She heard the sound of shovels digging in earth and crossed slowly to a pit. There, deep in the hole, stood Ethan, Simeon and Jonah. Emotion almost overcame Leah as she watched them scooping up soil and tossing it up to a pile heaped alongside the grave. "Ethan," she called quietly.

He looked up. Sweat poured down his face. His homespun shirt was limp and soaked. "Leah! What are you doing here?"

"I—I wanted to see you."

Ethan glanced at Jonah, who said, "Go."

Ethan came up a ladder and swung over the top edge of the hole. Leah stepped closer, but he stepped away. "I am dirty. I will mess you up." Dirt clung to his work boots and hands.

"Why are you doing this?"

"I want to. It is the very least I can do for her."

Leah realized that this was Ethan's way of easing his grief, of sweating off his own pain. The physical labor was good for him. She read it in his expression. "Is there something I can do to help?" she said. "Can I bring you water?"

Ethan shook his head. "We have water with us."

Leah shrugged and glanced around the cemetery. "Whose is the earliest grave?"

"Joseph Longacre. He was the infant son of my great-great-grandparents. He died one winter of scarlet fever."

"Sad," Leah said. "When babies die, it's really sad."

"Dying is part of living," Ethan said. "Nothing can bring my sister back to this life. Now she lives with God, in heaven. I know baby Joseph is playing with her."

Leah wanted to believe it too. How she wished to have Ethan's simple faith! But she was angry at God. He should have allowed Rebekah to live. "I guess I should go back to the house," Leah said.

"We will not be much longer," Ethan told her. "I will clean up and see you there. Many will come this afternoon and evening."

Leah returned to the house and stayed close to Charity. Later in the afternoon, Leah watched through the kitchen window as a lone black horse pulled a simple springboard wagon into the front yard. In the back of the wagon lay an unadorned child-sized pine coffin with two long poles attached to it. Six men, including Ethan, stepped up and pulled the coffin off the wagon, shouldered the poles and carried it up onto the porch, in through the front parlor, and into a small room at the back of the house.

Leah followed Charity and other family members into the room, a room swept meticulously clean, with only a table to hold the coffin, a single chair and a few candles. Both fascinated and repelled, Leah watched as the coffin was set upon the table turned bier. The window in the room was open, but without fans the room felt stifling. Leah left the small, airless room. She pressed herself against a wall, hoping not to faint from either the heat or her burden of grief.

Back in the kitchen, she splashed water on her face from the hand pump over the sink.

Minutes later, she felt Ethan's touch on her back. "More people are coming," he said, looking out the window. "To pay their respects."

Leah saw buggies pulling into the yard—a yard cleaned, weeded and clipped to receive friends and neighbors at its very best. Leah murmured, "I—I'm not sure I can go in there and look at her, Ethan."

"It does not matter. Only her body is in the coffin. Her spirit is with the Lord."

"There was a chair in the room. Why?"

"We will keep an all-night watch. It is our custom never to leave the body alone."

She wanted to ask why but decided he probably didn't know. He rarely knew the why of their customs, only that it was always done that way. She looked back to Ethan. "I think I should go."

"You do not have to."

Leah shook her head. "Yes, I do. I don't belong here. I'm the only English."

"That should not trouble you."

Tears filled her eyes. "But it does, Ethan. It does."

Ethan followed Leah outside. The undertaker had gone, but the memory of where his wagon had stood forced Leah to make a wide arc in the yard before she headed toward the road and her parked car. Ethan caught her elbow at the edge of the yard. "What will you do, Leah? Where are you going?"

"Back to my apartment, I guess." She wiped under her eyes. "I should start packing. There was a message on my answering machine from my mother when I got in last night. She and Neil are in Los Angeles and will be flying to Indianapolis today. She plans to come help me get my stuff home next week."

Ethan stared down at her. "I had forgotten. You will be leaving. But . . . so soon! I will miss you." The last was said haltingly, as if he was pulling the words from deep inside.

"You know, two weeks ago, the thought of leaving was driving me crazy." Leah looked over his shoulder at the rambling farmhouse. "Now . . . well, I'm sort of glad. It would be hard to stay, to expect to see Rebekah whenever I came out here." Her voice wavered. "It's best this way. I'll go back to my world. You'll stay in yours."

"You will always be a part of my world, Leah. Because you will always be a part of me."

Her gaze flew to his face. His clear blue eyes were serious, tinged with grief. Was some of it for her? For them? Leah choked down a sob, holding it at bay with steely resolve. "I have to go now. I don't think I can take any more sadness, Ethan. I can't."

He caught her arm once more. "Will you be here tomorrow?"

Leah nodded. "I have to come. I have to tell Rebekah goodbye."

"Yes," he said. "We will all tell her goodbye."

Yet as Leah drove off, she couldn't imagine watching that plain, undersized coffin being lowered into the cool, dark ground. She drove to town, weeping all the way.

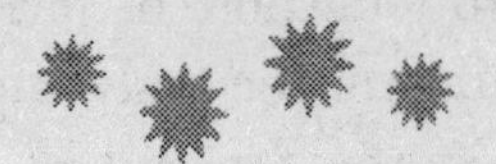

Twenty

It took Leah a long time to decide what to wear to Rebekah's funeral. Anxious that she might be the only English among the mourners, she didn't want to stand out any more than necessary. After much deliberation, she chose a simple black denim jumper and added a white T-shirt underneath. She brushed her dark hair and plaited it into a French braid. She wore no makeup, not even lip gloss.

She drove slowly to the farm, often following black buggies headed in the same direction. When she arrived, she saw a long line of buggies parked in the farmyard and along the country road fronting the farm. Younger kids helped with the horses, tying reins to hitching posts. Leah also took note of several cars. Glad not to have driven the only automobile, she again parked at the far end of the Longacre property and walked to the house. The first person that she saw in the yard and recognized by name was Martha Dewberry.

Martha's eyes were red from crying. "This is the worst thing that has ever happened," Martha said to Leah. "Rebekah was so sweet. So young."

Leah agreed. She felt no animosity toward Martha. There was no rivalry between them now. In the shared experience of grief, they were only two teenagers, mourning the loss of a friend. "I'll miss her," Leah said.

"She talked about you all the time. She thought you were glamorous." Martha managed a smile. "Like a movie star."

"You're kidding. I didn't know she even knew what a movie star was."

"She peeked in our magazines. The ones we stuff under our mattresses."

"My friends and I used to do the same thing," Leah said. "Hide the things we didn't want our parents to know about."

"It isn't easy growing up Amish. The things of the English are very tempting."

"Your Amish ways are tempting too," Leah said. "I guess neither way is easy."

Leah left Martha and slipped into the house. The furniture had been removed from the dining room and parlor. Wooden benches had been set in long rows. An usher, a young man Leah recognized from Jonah's group of friends, showed her to a place on one of the benches. Rebekah's coffin had been placed at the front of the room, and the Longacre family sat in front of the coffin with their backs to the rows of mourners.

As the mantel clock struck nine, a man stood, removed his hat, turned toward the others, and began to quote Scripture from the Old Testament. Eventually he mentioned Rebekah and the loss of her young life. But the man mostly talked to his audience about living godly lives and preparing themselves for eternal life. He quoted: " 'The Lord gave, and the Lord hath taken away; blessed be the name of the Lord.' " Leah thought it a strange eulogy.

At her grandmother's funeral, the minister had talked about Grandma Hall and her rich, full life. He'd mentioned how much she'd be missed and shared personal things about her life. Leah could only see the back of Ethan's head, but she wondered if he would have liked the minister to say more in praise of Rebekah. Leah certainly wished that the man had. But it wasn't her place to criticize, either.

Once the first man sat down, another stood and spoke. He also had little to say about Rebekah, but instead reminded all the Amish youth, "No person knows the hour of his death, so all must live good lives. Stay away from sinning." Leah shifted uncomfortably. Nothing either man said seemed to address the loss of Rebekah. She wondered if anyone was receiving comfort from these speeches.

Eventually the second man asked the group to kneel. He read a long prayer in German. Songs were not sung, but spoken in German. And just when Leah thought she couldn't sit for one more minute on the hard, uncomfortable bench, the congregation was asked to vacate the room. The room would be rearranged and the mourners would file past the coffin for one final farewell to Rebekah.

Leah almost panicked. She couldn't look at Rebekah. She couldn't! And yet, when the time came, she found herself in line in front of a young woman who was holding baby Nathan.

The child grabbed at Leah's braid, and Leah turned and smiled at him. The baby gave her a slobbery grin. The woman holding him spoke to him sternly, and Nathan's lower lip quivered.

Leah turned back toward the coffin, and with her heart hammering hard against her ribs, she stepped beside the plain pine box and looked down. The lid was formed in two halves. The top half was raised, and inside lay Rebekah. The child was dressed in white, the color for Amish mourning. Her head was covered with a white prayer cap, the ties fastened neatly beneath her chin. Leah wanted to untie them and let them hang loose, as Rebekah always had in life.

Leah's hands began to shake and her knees went weak. Rebekah looked waxen, like a store mannequin. From behind her, Leah heard Nathan squeal, "Bekah!" She turned to see him open his arms for his dead sister's hug.

The baby's lack of understanding unglued Leah completely. She bolted from the line and darted out the door. She pushed past people standing in the yard and, sobbing, started to run. Leah knew they were staring at her, but she didn't care. Blinded by her tears, she ran. She hit the boundary of the woods. Her heart was pounding, her lungs felt on fire. But she didn't stop running until she came to the great rock in the clearing where Ethan had brought her that moonlit night at the beginning of the summer.

Leah slumped against the great boulder, then slid to the ground. Fighting for breath, she buried her face in her hands. She knew she was missing the procession to the grave site. She knew she wasn't going to see them lower Rebekah's coffin into the ground and cover it with dirt. She didn't care. She couldn't watch anyway.

Slowly her sobs lessened. Her ragged breath calmed, and quiet settled all around her. Above her, she heard a faint breeze whispering through the pine needles. The faint scent of evergreens filled the air. And then she faintly heard someone say her name.

"Leah."

Expectantly she raised her head. Her breath caught in her throat. Less than fifty feet away, at the edge of the clearing, Leah saw Gabriella, dressed Amish. And beside Gabriella, Leah saw Rebekah. She wore the white dress Leah had seen in the coffin, and the prayer cap too. Except that the ties were loose and fluttering. In her hand, she held a lace-edged hanky. Rebekah's face looked radiant, as bright as sunshine. She raised her hand and gave an excited wave, and then, looking up at Gabriella, turned with her, walked away and disappeared behind the trees.

Stunned, stupefied, Leah took several seconds to react. She scrambled to her feet and raced into the woods, calling, "Rebekah! Gabriella! Where are you? Please, come back."

Leah spun in every direction, straining to see shapes in the thick foliage. Long shafts of sunlight hung in the air like yellow ribbons. A lone butterfly circled lazily over a cluster of wildflowers. Otherwise, Leah was alone. Gabriella was gone. Rebekah was gone. All that remained was the faint, sweet scent of pine.

Leah remained in the woods until she was certain the burial was over and the Amish neighbors had gone home. She kept trying to replay in her mind what she'd seen. *Gabriella. Rebekah. Holding hands.* They had had form and substance. They had not been ghosts, nor figments of her imagination. She'd seen them with her eyes wide open.

She left the woods and walked back to the house. Leah stepped up onto the porch and rapped gently on the door. Ethan came, and when he saw her, he opened the screen door wide. "I have been worried about you," he said. "I saw you run away. Where did you go? Are you all right?"

"Yes, Ethan. I'm all right now. I'm sorry I ran off. I've been in the woods. Can I talk to your parents?"

He glanced over his shoulder. "We are having Bible reading and prayer time. Maybe tomorrow would be better."

"It can't wait," Leah said, her heart pounding. "Please."

He took her into the parlor. The room was back in order, with no sign that a crowd of mourners had filled it only hours before. The family sat in a small circle. Baby Nathan played on the floor. Mr. Longacre closed the Bible on his lap and stood. His expression was one of deep sadness mixed with wariness and surprise. "We are in mourning, Leah."

Leah squared her shoulders. "I'm sorry to

barge in on you, but something happened today that I must tell you about." Quietly, her voice trembling, she told them what she'd seen in the woods. When she finished, she peered anxiously from face to face. The circle of eyes stared back at her. "Don't you believe me? Please tell me you believe me."

Mr. Longacre cleared his throat. "We have all had a great shock, Leah. Sometimes our minds play tricks on us."

"I tell you, I saw them both."

"Perhaps you fell asleep and dreamed this," Mrs. Longacre suggested with a quavery voice.

Leah shook her head vehemently. "I was wide awake. I saw Rebekah and Gabriella today. I know Rebekah told you about Gabriella and how Gabriella visited us in the hospital last December."

Mr. Longacre looked sterner than ever. "This is a hard thing to accept, Leah. The dead do not appear to the living. We will not see Rebekah again until we meet her in heaven."

Tears of frustration welled in Leah's eyes. How could she make them believe her? "I tell you, I *saw* her." Her voice sounded frantic to her own ears.

"Leah, stop!" Mr. Longacre commanded.

Ethan was by Leah's side instantly. "Papa, do not be angry. I know Leah. She would not make this up."

"Rebekah waved a hanky at me," Leah said, still desperate to make them believe her.

"You should go," Mr. Longacre said.

"Jacob, wait," Oma said, and everyone looked her way. She stood shakily, her face ashen. "I believe Leah. Early this morning, I had asked to spend a few minutes alone with Rebekah's coffin."

"*Ja.* I remember."

Oma's eyes were bright with tears. "I placed a hanky in her hand. I tucked it in carefully so that no one would see. It was a favorite of hers, and I wanted her to have it with her. No one could have known about the hanky except me. I acted as a foolish old woman, but she was such a precious child to me."

Leah felt suddenly giddy and as light as a feather. She wasn't going crazy. She had not imagined anything. "I—I saw her," Leah repeated softly. "I truly did."

The room was absolutely silent. Finally Jacob Longacre gave a slow nod. "So be it."

Tillie reached for Leah's hand. "Oh, Leah, God has given you a wonderful gift."

"Just as he did last Christmas," Charity added.

"You all believe me?" Leah asked again, relief draining her, making her very bones feel rubbery.

"What you have told us brings us peace," Mrs. Longacre said.

Tears started down Leah's cheeks. "Thank you," she said simply. She felt Ethan squeeze her hand. She turned, and, with head held high, left the room.

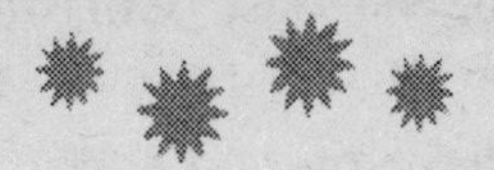

TWENTY-ONE

"I think that's about it." Neil slammed the back door of the rented moving trailer.

"I can't believe we got all your stuff into only two cars at the start of the summer," Leah's mother added. "Are you sure you don't mind driving back alone?"

Leah shook her head. "I don't mind."

Neil and her mother had driven up that morning, rented the trailer, and loaded Leah's things for the return trip home. It had been decided that Leah would follow in her car. By now it was late afternoon.

"I could ride with you," her mother said. "We haven't had a chance to catch up, and there's so much to tell you."

Leah glanced down the road leading from the parking lot of her apartment. Would Ethan come to say goodbye?

Neil caught Leah's eye and, with an understanding nod, took Leah's mother by the elbow. "There'll be plenty of time for that, honey, once we get home. Let's get going, and Leah can catch up. We'll be driving a whole lot slower anyway."

Leah tossed him a grateful glance. Neil must have realized that she was dragging her feet. "Sure, you two go on ahead and I'll be along. There are a couple more things I need to do."

Her mother frowned. "I can't imagine."

Leah had briefly mentioned Rebekah's death and funeral, and both Neil and her mother had been very sorry. Sympathy was all they could offer.

Neil opened the car door and guided his wife into the passenger seat. "Drive carefully," he called to Leah as he climbed into the car and started the engine.

"I won't be long," Leah promised. She watched them drive away, the trailer in tow. Alone in the parking lot, she felt foolish. She leaned against her car, unsure what to do.

The last time she'd seen Ethan, it had been at

the bus station with his family. They were going to visit an uncle in another part of the state. Mr. Longacre had thought that a short vacation would make them all feel better. Sarah and her husband, along with Jonah, would take care of the farm while they were gone. "My mom's coming next week to get me," Leah had told Ethan.

"I will see you before you leave," he'd promised her.

But the week had passed and he hadn't come. Leah couldn't put off leaving much longer. With only the stuffed bear Ethan had won for her at the fair and the lop-eared bunny glued to her dashboard, she had little else to remind her of him. She had no photos, no snapshots of their summer together. She had only memories.

She thought about driving to the farm for one last look but decided against it. She'd already said goodbye to the farm the day of Rebekah's funeral. With a sigh, she reached for the door handle.

"Leah! Wait!"

Leah whipped around and saw Ethan jogging down the side of the road toward her. She took off running, met him at the end of the block and threw herself into his arms. He scooped her up and hugged her hard against himself. He began kissing her face—her forehead, her cheeks, her eyelids, her mouth.

Leah clung to him, the sweetness of his lips almost melting her bones. "I was afraid you wouldn't make it."

Breathing heavily, Ethan set her back on her feet. "I had problems getting here. I caught the bus yesterday, but it broke down. They sent another bus, but not right away. When I got to the station, I started walking and running."

"I'm glad you made it. I didn't want to go off without saying goodbye."

"Me either."

He took her hand, led her across the street to a small public park, and sat with her on a green bench. A few kids were roller-skating on the sidewalk, and the clickety-clack of their skates over the cracks broke the silence of the warm summer day.

"How's your family doing?" Leah asked.

"We are getting over Rebekah's death slowly," he said solemnly. "Charity cries a lot, but Ma and Oma are there for her. Knowing what you saw in the woods brings us all much comfort."

Leah nodded. "Me too. I'll never get over her

dying, but I'm glad Gabriella let me see her one last time." Leah slipped her hand into his. "I really missed you while you were gone."

"All I thought about was you. Papa wasn't happy about my leaving early, but I do not care."

"Will you write me?"

"I will come and visit you."

"You will?" Her heart hammered. This was more than she had ever hoped for. "When?"

"When the harvest is in. I cannot leave Papa with so much work."

"Do you promise?"

Smiling down at her, Ethan asked, "Why do you want me to promise?"

"Because I know you always keep your word."

He kissed her warmly, deeply. "Do you not know, Leah? Do you not know that I love you?"

She started to cry. "I love you too. I have for months." She rested her cheek on his chest and felt the rough fabric of the homespun cloth. It gave her a jolt and instantly brought back all the differences between them. He was still Amish. She was still English. "What are we going to do, Ethan?"

"We are going to be together," he said.

"But—"

He silenced her with another kiss. "I do not know how, Leah. I do not know when. I only know we will."

Looking into Ethan's eyes, Leah believed him. His word was enough.

It was enough.

Coming soon:

When Angels Close My Eyes

Don't miss

Lurlene McDaniel's

heartrending and romantic new novels.

Despite a life-threatening illness, April has found the man of her dreams. Will they spend the rest of their lives together?

0-553-57085-4

0-553-57088-9

Getting over a lost love, April vacations with her parents and finds a kindred spirit. But will she be able to face the reoccurrence of her illness?